GENERATION ZERO

WE ARE THE FUTURE

FRED VAN LENTE | FRANCIS PORTELA | DEREK CHARM | ANDREW DALHOUSE

CONTENTS

Collection Cover Art: Stephen Mooney

Assistant Editor: Lauren Hitzhusen
Editor: Tom Brennan (#1-4)
Editor-in-Chief: Warren Simons

Generation Zero™: We Are the Future. Published by Valiant Entertainment LLC. Office of Publication: 350 Seventh Avenue, New York, NY 10001. Printed in the U.S.A. First Printing. ISBN: 9781682151754.

FRED VAN LENTE | FRANCIS PORTELA
ANDREW DALHOUSE

#1

GENERATION ZERO™

They are psiots - people born with the potential for incredible abilities of the mind. They were captured and trained by sinister corporate forces to become killing machines. They became one of the youngest strike forces on the planet. They broke free of their masters and, inspired by the heroism of their fellow psiots, the Harbinger Renegades, struck out on their own to make the world a better place. They will help you - if your cause is just. They are...

WE ARE THE FUTURE

CRONUS
STAY STRONG
STAY DEFIANT
Christian

TELIC
I KNEW YOU WERE
GOING TO ASK ME
TO WRITE THIS
—T

ANIMALIA
better to burn out
than to fade away

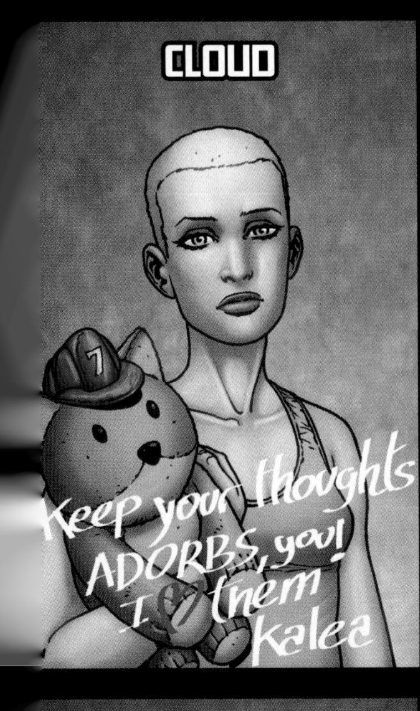
CLOUD
Keep your thoughts
ADORBS, you!
I ♡ them
Kalea

KEISHA
DISTRESSINGLY
NORMAL

GAMETE
SEE YOU NEXT
TRIMESTER!

ZYGOS TWINS (1/2)
We find your friendship acceptable

ZYGOS TWINS (2/2)
J&K

?
the BIG BAD?!?

"SO...
"...HOW DO I FIND THEM?"

WHAT?
I SAID HOW DO I FIND THEM?
POWERHOUSE ARENA, RIVER ROAD NW.
WHO?
YOU KNOW... THEM!
OH, YOU MEAN--
GIRL, THEY'RE JUST AN URBAN LEGEND!
LIKE SLENDERMAN-- OR DONALD TRUMP!
BUT I THOUGHT YOU TRIED--
YEAH, I WAS GONNA, BUT THEN I FELT SO STUPID-- LIKE A KID WRITING TO SANTA CLAUS--
OOOOH! HUSH UP, GIRL! I LOVE THIS SONG!

HOLOCADE, CASTLEMAN MALL.
MY STEPDAD, THE *SECOND* ONE? HE USED TO BE WITH D.O.D.--
--THAT'S DEPARTMENT OF DEFENSE--
I KNOW WHAT IT STANDS FOR, RHI...
33
HE SAID SOME REAL, LIKE, BASTARD-PEOPLE *MILITARY CONTRACTORS* GREW THE ZEROES IN A LAB TO BE HUMAN WEAPONS. BUT THEN THEY *ESCAPED,* AND...
OMG. REMEMBER WHEN, LIKE, THAT CITY IN MEXICO BLEW UP?
YOU MEAN *MEXICO* CITY?
THAT'S THE ONE!
MY SECOND STEPDAD SAYS *THEY* DID THAT. SOMEONE CALLED THEM THERE, AND THEY JUST LEVELED THE PLACE. TO THE GROUND.
BUT *HOW* WERE THEY CALLED?
WHO KNOWS? IT DOESN'T MATTER, *NOW.*
THEY WERE IN THE MIDDLE OF THAT EXPLOSION! THEY'RE DEADER THAN *DISCO,* KEISHA.

9:41 AM
Ir a la versión web
Fin de la cita
MENÚ
NOTICIAS MARIANAS.es
¡DESASTRE!
ROOK HIGH SCHOOL, LAZARUS LANE SE.
HELL, GIRL.
WHAT I HEARD?
GO ON...
THEY FIND YOU.
GO ON BABBLE®?
SET THE CHAT CHANNEL TO ZERO?
THEY DON'T HELP EVERYBODY.
IN FACT, THEY HELP ALMOST NOBODY.
ALL YOU CAN DO?

SHERMAN HOUSE, PINE STREET SW.
"MAKE YOUR CASE.
"THEN THEY DECIDE WHETHER TO COME OR NOT."
NOFX
DO VASES HAVE EYES
LA LLORONA
BABBLE
#ZERO
OKAY. OKAY.
I'VE TRIED EVERYTHING ELSE.
SO I'VE GOT NOTHING TO LOSE BUT MY DIGNITY...
KLICK
ERO
GO

SEE THIS, ZEROES?
SEE WHAT HAPPENS WHEN THEY TALK CRAP ABOUT ME? SEE WHAT I DO?!
IT'S LIKE THEIR WORDS CUT ME THEM-SELVES.
COULD YOU...COULD YOU TELL MY PARENTS?
THAT I WAS BORN IN A BODY NOT MY OWN.
MY MOM... SHE WILL KILL ME IF I TELL HER. I KNOW.
SHE'LL SAY IT'S WHAT THE LORD WOULD WANT.
HELLO, UH... OUT THERE...MY NAME IS KEISHA SHERMAN?
I'M CALLING FROM...ROOK, MICHIGAN? Y'KNOW, THE MICHIGAN MIRACLE?
IF YOU DON'T GET HARRIS TO STOP--
--I'M GONNA STOP HIM. ANY WAY I CAN.
I FOUND THE COMBO TO DAD'S GUN SAFE... AND I CAN... I CAN...
THEY FOUND US--WE WERE IN MY CAR--PARKED AT THE END OF A CUL-DE-SAC--
--AND THEY ARRESTED US! AND NOW--BECAUSE MY GIRLFRIEND IS 15--
THEY SAY I'M GONNA GO ON THE SEX OFFENDER LIST! THAT'S GOING TO RUIN MY WHOLE LIFE!
IS THERE-- PLEASE TELL ME THERE'S SOMETHING YOU CAN DO FOR ME, ZEROES?

ROOK
"ANDERSON COOPER CAME UP WITH THAT 'MIRACLE' NAME ON THE NEWS.
"I GUESS THERE USED TO BE A LOT OF FACTORIES HERE? AND JOBS? BEFORE THERE WEREN'T, I MEAN?
"BUT THE STATE STEPPED IN, APPOINTED, A WHAT DO YOU CALL IT, "EMERGENCY MANAGER," WHATEVER...
"...AND HE TURNED IT AROUND. ROOK GOT ANOTHER NAME THEN."
"REDNECK DUBAI."
OUR TOWN GETS THE BEST OF EVERYTHING. ALL THE BEST BANDS... THE HOLOGRAM ARCADE... (OH AND TOWNWIDE FREE WIFI...)
...BECAUSE NOW WE CAN AFFORD IT.
"OUR SCHOOL HAS THE CUTTING EDGE OF THE CUTTING EDGE IN 'LEARNING-IS-NOT-BORING-NO-REALLY-IT-ISN'T' TECH...
"EVERYBODY LOVES IT.
"EVERYBODY GETS WITH THE PROGRAM."

"EVERYBODY...
EXCEPT STEPHEN.
"MY LAST NAME IS SHERMAN, AND HIS WAS SEO, SO WE GOT SEATED NEXT TO EACH OTHER IN CLASS.
"THE NOTES STARTED.
U LIKE ME?!?
"THEN THE TEXTS.
INCOMING: STEPHEN
- CAN'T STOP THINKING ABOUT YOU
- THAT'S WEIRD RIGHT
- BECAUSE I DON'T WANT TO STOP
- AND THAT'S WEIRDER
"THEN THE REALITY."

FIREWATCH TOWER, LOOKOUT PARK.
"HE WAS DIFFERENT. HE COULD SEE WHAT THE OTHERS DIDN'T.
"HE COULD TELL."
THIS TOWN IS SO FAKE. LIKE A...WHAT WAS MR. ITO TALKING ABOUT IN WORLD HISTORY?
A POTEMKIN VILLAGE? JUST A BUNCH OF FLATS OR WHATEVER...
...YEAH, ALL FOR SHOW.
A PHONY TOWN FOR PHONY PEOPLE.
I'VE BEEN... WELL. I THINK I'VE FIGURED OUT WHO THE SHOW IS FOR...
WHAT IS IT? WHAT'S THE BIG SECRET?
SOON... I'LL TELL YOU SOON...JUST AS SOON AS I KNOW FOR SURE...
...THEN WE CAN FINALLY BE FREE OF THIS DUMP...
...AND BE TOGETHER, FOREVER...

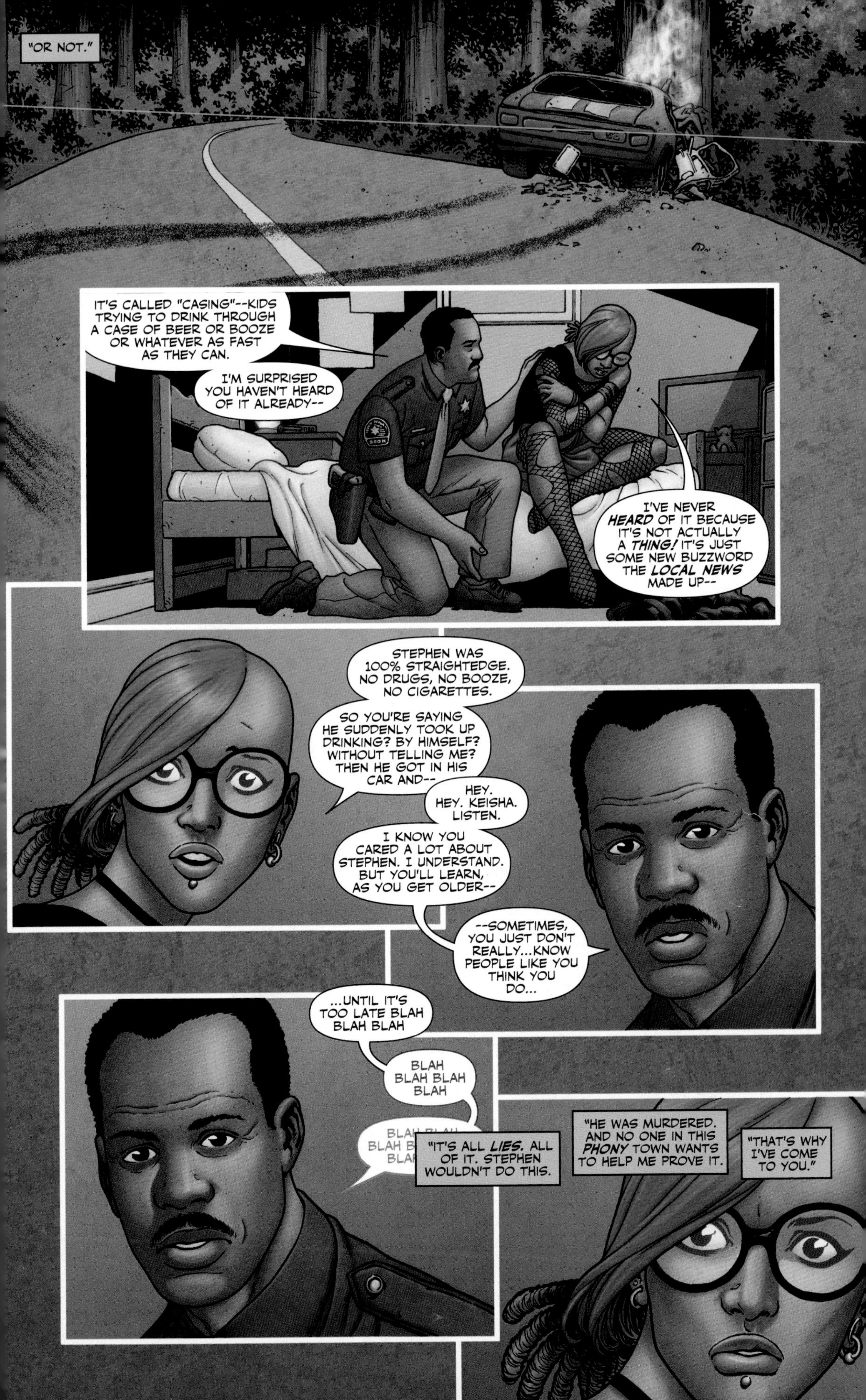

"OR NOT."
IT'S CALLED "CASING"--KIDS TRYING TO DRINK THROUGH A CASE OF BEER OR BOOZE OR WHATEVER AS FAST AS THEY CAN.
I'M SURPRISED YOU HAVEN'T HEARD OF IT ALREADY--
I'VE NEVER HEARD OF IT BECAUSE IT'S NOT ACTUALLY A THING! IT'S JUST SOME NEW BUZZWORD THE LOCAL NEWS MADE UP--
STEPHEN WAS 100% STRAIGHTEDGE. NO DRUGS, NO BOOZE, NO CIGARETTES.
SO YOU'RE SAYING HE SUDDENLY TOOK UP DRINKING? BY HIMSELF? WITHOUT TELLING ME? THEN HE GOT IN HIS CAR AND--
HEY. HEY. KEISHA. LISTEN.
I KNOW YOU CARED A LOT ABOUT STEPHEN. I UNDERSTAND. BUT YOU'LL LEARN, AS YOU GET OLDER--
--SOMETIMES, YOU JUST DON'T REALLY...KNOW PEOPLE LIKE YOU THINK YOU DO...
...UNTIL IT'S TOO LATE BLAH BLAH BLAH
BLAH BLAH BLAH BLAH
"IT'S ALL LIES. ALL OF IT. STEPHEN WOULDN'T DO THIS.
"HE WAS MURDERED. AND NO ONE IN THIS PHONY TOWN WANTS TO HELP ME PROVE IT.
"THAT'S WHY I'VE COME TO YOU."

KEISHA SHERMAN.

CRAP!

YOU HAVE SUCCESSFULLY MADE CONTACT WITH **GENERATION ZERO.**
DO NOT TELL ANYBODY ABOUT THIS COMMUNICATION.
DESTROY WHATEVER DEVICE IS RECEIVING THIS TRANSMISSION IMMEDIATELY.

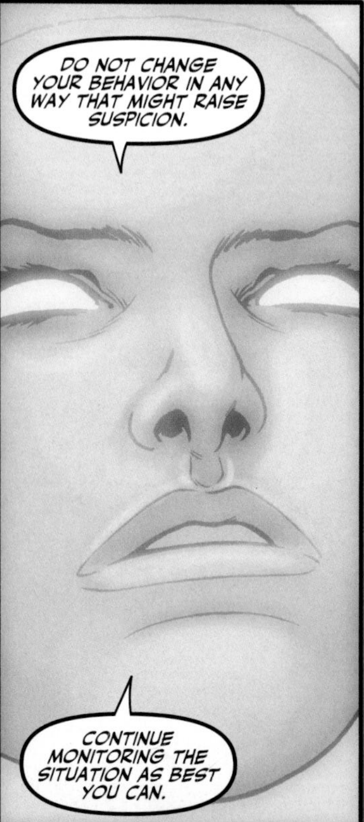

DO NOT CHANGE YOUR BEHAVIOR IN ANY WAY THAT MIGHT RAISE SUSPICION.
CONTINUE MONITORING THE SITUATION AS BEST YOU CAN.

YOUR REQUEST HAS BEEN PLACED INTO THE QUEUE FOR PROPER HANDLING.
WE WILL RESPOND TO IT AS QUICKLY AS WE CAN.

DO NOT ATTEMPT TO MAKE CONTACT WITH US AGAIN.
BLLLLPP
WELL, CRAP.
SIGH
DAAAAAAAAAAAAD?
KEISHA, YOU STILL UP? EVERYTHING OKAY?
MOSTLY... JUST...
MY LAPTOP DIED! I'M GONNA NEED A NEW ONE!
AW, C'MON, GIRL! YOU'RE JOKING!
YOU'RE MAKING ME WEAR OUT THE TRAIL BETWEEN HERE AND BEST BUY...
WE CAN AFFORD IT, NOW!
YOU'VE GOT TO BE MORE CAREFUL WITH YOUR THINGS! JUST BECAUSE WE CAN AFFORD TO BUY SOMETHING DOESN'T MEAN WE SHOULD.
GO CHECK ON YOUR BROTHER, OKAY? TIME FOR BED.
OK, DAD.

HEY, KWAME.
ALMOST READY TO WRAP IT UP?
TIME FOR BED!
OKAY, KEISHA. THIS IS THE LAST ONE.
NEVER CEASES TO BLOW ME AWAY THAT YOU CAN DO THAT BY HAND...

I HAVE NO CHOICE.
DAD LEFT THE SPIROGRAPH SET BEHIND IN THE MOVE.
THERE. COULD YOU FIND A SPOT FOR THIS ONE THE WALL?
IT'LL CONFUSE *THE CORNERMEN,* BECAUSE--
--THEY CAN ONLY MOVE THROUGH RIGHT ANGLES, YEAH, I REMEMBER.
THE DAMN WHATEVER-MEN WON'T BE ABLE TO GET YOU WHILE I'M AROUND, BRO.
IT'S NOT REALLY UP TO YOU, THOUGH. YOU CAN'T EVEN SEE THEM IF YOU DON'T HAVE WEAPONIZED GEOMETRY.
UH-HUH. SURE...
KEISHA...
WHAT IS IT BABY?
DID I SAY I WAS SORRY ABOUT STEPHEN?
I...
I MEAN, I'M SURE YOU DID.
I KNOW HE MEANT THINGS TO YOU.
I MEAN, I DON'T KNOW WHAT *THAT* MEANS, BUT I KNOW IT'S IMPORTANT.
SO I'M SORRY.
THANKS, KID.
I LOVE YOU.
GOOD NIGHT.

"MONITOR" THE SITUATION, SHE SAID...I GUESS I CAN DO THAT...
HAVE FUN AT SCHOOL TODAY, KWAME!
WE'RE NOT DOING THE WAVING THING, HUH?
THAT'S PEACHY.
THE "SITUATION" IS, I AM ONE OF THE OUTLIERS. THE PUNKS. THE GOTHS. THE STONERS.
BUT OUR NUMBERS KEEP DWINDLING.
GETTING ABSORBED... BY THE "IN-CROWD."
THE FILTY RICH KIDS--THE KIDS OF THE CEO'S AND R&DS OF THE COMPANIES THAT RUN THE NEW ROOK--THEY USED TO LOOK AT ME WITH CONTEMPT...
...NOW IT'S JUST PITY.
I CAN READ IT IN ALL THEIR EYES.
"THE GIRL WHOSE LOVE DIED."

OH, HEY-- KESH! I ALMOST FORGOT!
YOU KNOW-- HOPEFULLY YOU CAN MAKE IT! IF THAT'S COOL?
THIS THURSDAY? YEAH, I'LL SEE-- THANKS...
WOW. HAS ADELE EVEN TALKED TO YOU BEFORE?
I DIDN'T THINK SHE KNEW MY NAME...
SHE HAS LITERALLY INVITED YOU TO A PITY PARTY.
KEYS CLUB PARTY FOR STEPHEN
WELL...WITH THAT BOYCOTT OF WHOLE FOODS AND HER CAMPAIGN FOR THE CHEERLEADING TEAM TO HOST A SYRIAN REFUGEE...
...I'M JUST ANOTHER CHECK MARK OFF "WHY I CAN KEEP THINKING I'M A GOOD PERSON."
YOU GONNA LET HER EXPLOIT YOU FOR HER OWN FEELS?
I DON'T KNOW YET. ON THE ONE HAND: MY PERSONAL INTEGRITY.
ON THE OTHER: FREE BEER.
TRULY, A MORAL QUANDARY FOR THE AGES.

WHERE YOU HEADED KWAME?
ROOM.
SHERMAN
DON'T DO ANYTHING I WOULDN'T DO, PARTY ANIMAL...
OH MY...
OH MY GOD...
HE SENT THIS...BY THE POST OFFICE. BEFORE HE DIED!
from
STEPHEN SEO
ECHIDNA ST. #14
ROOK, MI 15028
KEISHA SHERMAN
PINE ST.
ROOK, MI 15028
NOT DIGITAL. NOT ANY WAY ONE COULD EASILY TRACK.
MIGHT AS WELL HAVE USED A CARRIER PIGEON.
AND A CD...HE MIGHT AS WELL HAVE SENT IT BY SEMAPHORE.
KESH'S MIX
OH, YEAH.

KESH'S

HEY, KEISHA. SORRY ABOUT ALL THE CREEPERY.
HIS VOICE...
IF YOU'RE GETTING THIS...IT'S BECAUSE I DIDN'T WANT TO RISK YOUR LIFE WITHOUT BEING **SURE.**

THE MESSED-UP THING IS...I'M PRETTY SURE MY OWN **PARENTS** ARE INVOLVED--ALL OF OURS ARE--I CAN'T **TRUST** THEM.
I CAN'T, I JUST CAN'T...
YOU CAN'T TRUST YOURS EITHER! I CAN'T PROTECT YOU...

I'M GONNA LOSE IT...
...UNLESS I EXPOSE THEIR **SECRET**--IT'S IN THE SLURRY POND, JUST OUTSIDE TOWN.

THE POND?
THAT'S WHERE THE **SECOND TOWER** IS. I CAN HEAR IT CALLING TO ME, IN MY SLEEP...

I'M GONNA DROP THIS IN THE MAIL AND THEN DRIVE OVER HERE...

HOPEFULLY WE CAN LISTEN TO IT TOGETHER AND LAUGH OUR ASSES OFF THAT I EVER THOUGHT I'D NEED TO **DO** THIS...
THE ***POND...***
CAN'T GET OVER THERE WITHOUT SOME CREEPERY OF MY OWN...

CLICK
QR CODE ON THE INVITE PINS COORDINATES TO THE KEGGER IN YOUR MAPS.
THEN YOU BURN THE INVITE SO THE KEYS CAN KEEP THE UNDESIRABLES OUT.
LIKE ME, UP UNTIL VERY VERY RECENTLY.
THEY CAN'T STOP LOOKING AT ME, AND HATE THEMSELVES FOR IT.
HEY KEISHA!
HEY!
HEY KEISHA, YOUR DAD KNOW YOU'RE HERE? SNORT
C'MON, DON'T BE A...
BOY, IT'S TRUE WHAT THEY SAY.
FOOTBALL CONCUSSION DAMAGE BEGINS EARLY.
HEY! THAT'S A REAL DISABILITY!

BISHOP'S WOODS.
MAKES TWO OF US.
'SUP!
HEY.
KEISHA! I'M SO GLAD YOU MADE IT!
HEY, ADELE.
HOLD MY HAIR ALL THE WAY BACK, TROLL.
HLLLLRRGG!
UGH, THE TASTE-- WHO CAN DRINK THIS STUFF?
WHO'S YOUR DAD?
WHAT?

WHY'D THEY ASK YOU IF YOUR DAD KNEW YOU WERE HERE?
HE'S THE SHERIFF. MY DAD.
HUH. THAT'S FUNNY.
TO THEM, MAYBE.
HE'S CUTE.
REALLY CUTE.
BUT HE'S ALREADY GOT A HAREM.
WHAT'S YOUR NAME?
KEISHA. YOU'RE NOT FROM AROUND HERE, ARE YOU?
NOT UNTIL TODAY. STARTING SCHOOL TOMORROW.
IF YOU WEREN'T IN SCHOOL, HOW'D YOU HEAR ABOUT THIS KEYS PARTY?
WE'RE HARD TO KEEP SECRETS FROM.
IS THAT RIGHT?
THAT IS.
I'M CHRISTIAN, BY THE WAY.
IS THAT YOUR NAME, OR ARE YOU ANNOUNCING YOUR PERSONAL BELIEF SYSTEM?

NAME.
GOOD. MOST PEOPLE LEAD WITH THAT.
MY PERSONAL BELIEF SYSTEM IS...
...FUNGIBLE.
OOH, GOOD S.A.T. WORD.
A LITTLE YOUNG FOR A KEYS CLUB PARTY, RIGHT?
NO.
WELL COULD YOU STOP, UH, STARING AT ME SO MUCH? IT'S MAKING ME UNCOMFORTABLE.
THAT'S THE IDEA.
THAT'S MY CUE...
AW, C'MON, THAT'S JUST MONICA BEING MONICA...
NAH. I'M GONNA GO OVER HERE.
CARS ARE BACK THERE.
I KNOW. GOTTA TINKLE.
LADYLIKE OF YOU.
YEAH, I'M JANE AUSTEN'S WET DREAM.
I'VE GOT A NAME FOR YOU, CHRISTIAN, WHOEVER YOU ARE.
AND IT'S "TOO SOON."

SICK OF WAITING FOR THESE ZEROES.
PROBABLY IS JUST A BIG SCAM, ANYWAY. OR SOME KIND OF ELABORATE VIRAL PR STUNT.
I CAN NANCY DREW THIS MYSELF.
HERE WE ARE...FORTUNATELY THE PARTY WAS NEARBY, TO PROVIDE ME COVER...
...THE WASTE OUTFLOW OF ROOK'S COLLECTIVE MIRACLE BUSINESSES.
SMELLS LIKE A GIANT URINAL PUCK.
WHAT DID STEPHEN EXPECT TO FIND HERE?
THIS...IS GOING TO BE LIKE ONE OF THOSE VIDEO GAMES, RIGHT?
ONE OF THOSE VIDEO GAMES WHERE YOU NEVER DIE, AND ALL THE CLUES ARE PROMINENTLY DISPLAYED IN WIDESCREEN VIEW, BECAUSE YOU HAVE SPECIAL VISION THAT MAKES ANYTHING RELEVANT TO YOUR STORYLINE AUTOMATICALLY APPEAR, RIGHT...?
AND ESPECIALLY WHERE YOU NEVER DIE.
RIGHT...?

ACE WHITENERS, HIM A HO MUSKS.
OH MY...
OH...
A HUNTED TOWN WOO TRYOUT.

BEHAVE WIFE WILLOW TUT!
CHUM CHUM CHUM
NO! NO WAY!
AAHHH!
SSKRTCH
I HEARD YOUR WHOLE LIFE FLASHES BEFORE YOUR EYES...
...BUT INSTEAD, I JUST SEE STEPHEN.
AND THAT'S RIGHT...
...TO SEE HIS GHOST...
WAIT--NO--NOT A GHOST--
--A BLUR--
ZWOKK

THEN-- A SOUND--
SHRAKKKKKKKK
--LIKE SOMEONE PUNCHED A HOLE IN THE *WORLD*--
HIS HOW OW!
FORENOON OUTS...
AND, THEN, ALL OF A SUDDEN.
I CAN'T THINK
OF A SINGLE
CLEVER
THING
TO SAY
IT'S ALL RIGHT NOW.
YOU *CALLED* FOR US.

AND GENERATION ZERO *CAME.*

VALIANT | FRED VAN LENTE | FRANCIS PORTELA
ANDREW DALHOUSE

#2

GENERATION ZERO™

WE ARE THE FUTURE.

BISHOP'S WOODS
JUST OUTSIDE OF ROOK, MI
I CALLED "GENERATION ZERO" BECAUSE SOMEONE KILLED MY BOYFRIEND--BECAUSE I THOUGHT THEY COULD HELP.
HECK ARE THESE THINGS, CRONUS? I'M NOT GETTING ANY READ ON THEM.
GEOMANCY?
PSIOT-DAMPENERS?
TIMEARC DEPOSITS?
ALIEN TECHNOLOGY?
BECAUSE I THOUGHT THEY WOULD UNDERSTAND ME.
AW MAN, NOT ALIENS AGAIN.
ALIENS SMELL SO WEIRD.
BUT NOW THEY'RE HERE... EVEN THOUGH THEY SAVED MY LIFE...MAYBE I'M THE ONE WHO DOESN'T UNDERSTAND.
THEY LOOK LIKE YOU OR ME.
GEEZ, ANIMALIA, THAT IS SO RACIST.
NUH-UH NO IT'S NOT, TELIC!
IT'S SPECIESIST.
THEY TALK LIKE YOU OR ME.
MY BROTHER...
BUT THEY'RE...NOT LIKE YOU OR ME.
...HE CALLS THEM "CORNERMEN."

THERE'S SOMETHING...I DON'T KNOW, WILD ABOUT THEM, THE WAY THEY CARRY THEMSELVES. LIKE THEY HAVE NO WEIGHT.
YOUR BROTHER? WHAT DOES HE KNOW ABOUT THEM?
HE--WELL, HE IS ON THE SPECTRUM. SPECTRUMS. SPECTRA.
RUBBER PEOPLE... EEWWWW...
I-I WASN'T SURE WHAT HE MEANT WHEN HE WARNED ME ABOUT PEOPLE WHO USE "WEAPONIZED GEOMETRY"... BUT I GUESS HE WAS BEING LITERAL.
IF IT'S TRUE-- IF THIS REALLY IS GENERATION ZERO--THEN THEY'RE CAPABLE OF DOING ANYTHING.
THEY'RE DANGEROUS BUT... BEAUTIFUL, TOO...
MAYBE, KEISHA.
THAT ARM DOESN'T LOOK SO GOOD. I SHOULD TAKE A LOOK AT IT--
BUT-- UH--WHY? I SAW YOU BLAST THOSE HOODED DUDES INTO SMITHEREENS WITH THAT HAND!
...LIKE A FLAME.
WELL. HERE'S THE THING:
THE SAME ENERGY MY BODY GENERATES CAN HEAL AS WELL AS HARM.
SEE?
OH!
THAT FEELS...
WOW.
FEELS LIKE ICY HOT.

THIS IS THE SHERIFF. DO NOT MOVE.
WHOOP
KEEP YOUR HANDS WHERE I CAN SEE THEM.
AND STEP TOWARD THE LIGHT.
...
KEISHA?
BABY?
IS THAT YOU?
HEY, DAD...
GOT CALLED TO BREAK UP ANOTHER OF ADELE POOLE'S KEYS CLUB PARTIES...ON A SCHOOL NIGHT, FOR CHRISSAKES...
...AND THEY TOLD US QUITE A COMMOTION WAS BEING KICKED UP DOWN BY THE SLURRY POND...
DON'T TELL ME YOU'RE MIXED UP WITH THAT GIRL'S NONSENSE, KEISHA. I DON'T NEED TO REMIND YOU WHO HER FATHER IS. SHE'S PROTECTED...
ME? OH, NO. NO. ME AND MY FRIENDS... WE WERE JUST CHILLING...
"FRIENDS," HUH?

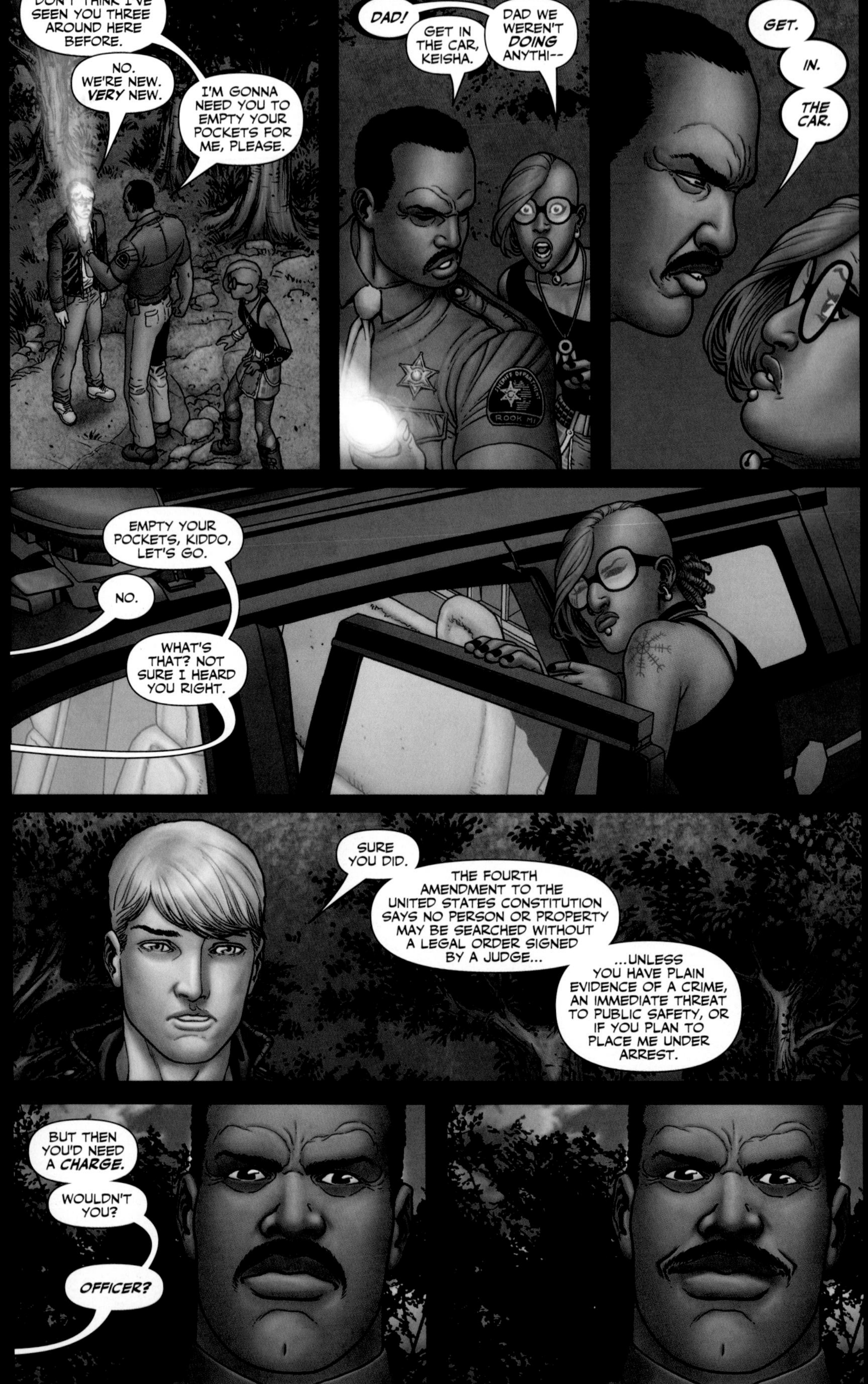
DON'T THINK I'VE SEEN YOU THREE AROUND HERE BEFORE.
NO. WE'RE NEW. *VERY* NEW.
I'M GONNA NEED YOU TO EMPTY YOUR POCKETS FOR ME, PLEASE.
DAD!
GET IN THE CAR, KEISHA.
DAD WE WEREN'T *DOING* ANYTHI--
SHERIFF DEPARTMENT
ROOK MI
GET.
IN.
THE CAR.
EMPTY YOUR POCKETS, KIDDO, LET'S GO.
NO.
WHAT'S THAT? NOT SURE I HEARD YOU RIGHT.
SURE YOU DID.
THE FOURTH AMENDMENT TO THE UNITED STATES CONSTITUTION SAYS NO PERSON OR PROPERTY MAY BE SEARCHED WITHOUT A LEGAL ORDER SIGNED BY A JUDGE...
...UNLESS YOU HAVE PLAIN EVIDENCE OF A CRIME, AN IMMEDIATE THREAT TO PUBLIC SAFETY, OR IF YOU PLAN TO PLACE ME UNDER ARREST.
BUT THEN YOU'D NEED A *CHARGE.*
WOULDN'T YOU?
OFFICER?

SPREAD YOUR LEGS.
WHUMMP
SPREAD 'EM.
STAND DOWN, ANIMALIA.
THAT'S AN ORDER.
NO WALLET. NO I.D.
NO CASH.
NO CAR KEYS. NO HOUSE KEYS.
NO CELL PHONE.
YOU SURE YOU NEW IN TOWN...
...OR JUST... PASSING THROUGH?

MMMM-HM. WE LIKE TO KEEP ROOK A NICE TOWN.
SO THERE'S A CURFEW FOR KIDS UNDER EIGHTEEN. ELEVEN P.M.
THIS I DID NOT KNOW. THANKS FOR CLUING US IN, SHERIFF.
YEAH, WELL, DON'T FORGET IT.
NEED A LIFT?
NO, THANK YOU, MY SISTERS AND I WILL WALK. IT'S NOT FAR.
AND KID...
CHRISTIAN.
OH, I WON'T NEED TO REMEMBER YOUR NAME.
BECAUSE I'M NOT GONNA SEE YOU ANYWHERE NEAR MY DAUGHTER EVER AGAIN.
AM I?
MAN. THIS TOWN...
YEAH...
...THEY'RE NEVER GONNA KNOW WHAT HIT IT.

DAD...THAT WAS SO EMBARRASSING...
KEISHA, BABY...
I WANNA THANK YOU.
THANK ME...? WHY?
FOR BEING SO... UNDERSTANDING ABOUT THIS TRANSITION.
I KNOW IT STUNK TO LEAVE SAN JOSÉ, ALL YOUR FRIENDS, YOUR SCHOOL...
AND YOU TAKE SUCH GOOD CARE OF YOUR BROTHER.
SINCE YOUR MOTHER...I MEAN, LOOKING AFTER KWAME, THAT WAS ALWAYS HER JOB.
I WISH I COULD HELP OUT MORE, BE AROUND MORE, BUT--EMERGENCY MANAGER POOLE EXPECTS A LOT OF ME.
WE SERVED IN FALLUJAH TOGETHER, BUT THAT ONLY GETS SO FAR. I GOTTA PROVE I'M THE BEST MAN FOR THIS JOB.
I GOTTA WORK TWICE AS HARD AS THE SHERIFF BEFORE ME, AND YOU'RE OLD ENOUGH TO KNOW WHY.
THIS TOWN IS THE FUTURE. IT CAN BE OUR FUTURE, AND A GOOD ONE.
I CAN'T TELL YOU HOW MUCH IT MEANS TO ME YOU'RE HELPING ME OUT LIKE THIS, BABY.
THAT'S WHY IT BURNS ME UP WHEN I SEE YOU GETTING MIXED UP WITH PUNKS LIKE THAT KID.
THERE'S NOTHING WRONG WITH THEM, DAD! THEY'RE MY FRIENDS!

BABY GIRL, LOOK, I KNOW BAD NEWS BEARS WHEN I SEE 'EM.
I MEAN, THEY'RE IN A "FOSTER FAMILY?" THEY OPEN A HALFWAY HOUSE FOR JUVENILE DELINQUENTS IN ROOK? I DON'T THINK SO.
THERE IS NO WAY JASON POOLE WOULD SIGN OFF ON THAT...
WHAT THE-- WHAT IS THIS CRAP?
WHAT'S WRONG?!
WHEN I CATCH THAT SMUG LITTLE P.O.S. I WILL SLAP THE SMUG RIGHT OFF OF HIM!
58★582
SHERIFF

ROOK HIGH SCHOOL.
KEISHA SHERMAN, PLEASE REPORT TO THE VICE PRINCIPAL'S OFFICE...
GREAT, SO THE ZEROES DID RESPOND TO MY CALL AND COME TO HELP ME.
NOW WHAT?
WE'RE NO CLOSER TO FINDING OUT WHY MY BOYFRIEND WAS KILLED THAN I WAS BEFORE THEY SHOWED UP...
...I TRIED TALKING TO KWAME ABOUT "CORNERMEN" BUT HE WAS EVEN LESS RESPONSIVE THAN USUAL...
...THE SLURRY POND WAS A DEAD END... JUST A TRAP FOR STEPHEN AND ME...
SHERMAN... KEISHA SHERMAN...TO THE VICE PRINCIPAL'S OFFICE...
CHRISTIAN
STIAN
CHRISTIA
CHRISTIAN
CH
CHR
YES! ONE-POINT CONVERSION!
DOINK
OW!
DUNH-DUNH! YOU GO DEAF OVERNIGHT, MS. LAW AND ORDER? THEY'RE PLAYING YOUR SONG!
JESUS, DRAKE, HAS ANYONE IN THEIR ENTIRE LIFE EVER MADE THE MISTAKE OF CALLING YOU FUNNY...?
SHERMAN... SHERMAN TO THE VEEP... COME IN, KEISHA SHERMAN...
THEY'RE GONNA GIVE HER HER NEXT NARC-ING ASSIGNMENT... CHUCKLE
I'LL WRITE DOWN WHATEVER YOU MISS IN FIRST PERIOD, KEESH.
THANKS, RHI, I APPRECIATE IT...

I MEAN...THE ZEROES *DISAPPEARED* JUST AS QUICKLY AS THEY *ARRIVED*...

...THEY CLAIM THEY'RE *"ON THE CASE"* BUT I DON'T KNOW WHAT THEY'RE DOING...OR HOW I CAN CONTACT THEM IF I NEED TO TELL ANYTHING...

I MEAN...I'M THE *CLIENT* HERE, RIGHT?

SHOULDN'T *I* BE IN ON THE *GAME PLAN?*

AH, MS. SHERMAN. AT LAST! COME IN.

I'D LIKE YOU TO MEET THE NEWEST MEMBERS OF THE ROOK HIGH COMMUNITY:

JAMES AND KATHERINE ZYGOS. THEIR ADMISSION EXAM RESULTS WERE OFF THE CHARTS, SO THEY'VE SKIPPED A FEW GRADES TO JOIN OUR FRESHMAN CLASS.

WOULD YOU BE THEIR ***UPPERCLASSMAN MENTOR*** AND SHOW THEM AROUND THE SCHOOL WHILE I SETTLE SOME PAPERWORK WITH THEIR MOTHER DIANA, HERE?

HELLO, KEISHA SHERMAN.
YES, HELLO, KEISHA SHERMAN.
WE ACCEPT YOUR OFFER OF FRIENDSHIP.

YOU'RE... YOU'RE WITH THEM, RIGHT? THE ZEROES? THAT'S NOT YOUR REAL MOTHER IS IT? CHRISTIAN'S MOTHER--?
NO, OF COURSE NOT.
THAT IS GAMETE'S MOTHER.
GAMETE?

"YES, ANIMALIA NAMED HER GAMETE THE SUPER-FETUS."
I SEE YOU COME TO OUR LITTLE TOWN FROM MEXICO CITY, MS. AGUILAR...
...I HOPE YOU KNOW I SPEAK FOR ALL AMERICANS WHEN I SAY I AM SO SORRY FOR YOUR CITY AND YOUR LOSS.
THANK YOU, MRS. VICE PRINCIPAL. ALL I CAN SAY IS, I FEEL THE PRESENCE OF THOSE WE LOST IN THEIR ABSENCE...
...AND IT'S WHAT KEEPS ME GOING EVERY DAY.
"DIANA MARIA AGUILAR WAS KNOCKED INTO A COMA WHEN HER CITY WAS FIRST ATTACKED."
I'M SORRY, I DIDN'T QUITE CATCH THAT? I DON'T KNOW IF IT'S YOUR ACCENT...
...OR THE FACT YOUR LIPS DON'T REALLY MOVE...
NO NEED TO CONCERN YOURSELF WITH THAT.
LET'S GET MY FOSTER CHILDREN REGISTERED AND READY FOR SCHOOL.
"AND HER PSIOT DAUGHTER HAS NOT SHOWN ANY INCLINATION TO COME OUT SINCE. FORTUNATELY FOR US."
RIGHT. SO THEY'RE... ADOPTED, YES?
AND YOU HAVE ALL THE PROPER STATE AND LOCAL PAPERWORK?
NO. I DO NOT.
BUT YOU DON'T REALLY NEED TO SEE THAT.
DO YOU?
"IT IS HIGHLY USEFUL TO HAVE SOMEONE WHO PASSES AS AN ADULT ON THE FIRETEAM."
YOU KNOW WHAT, THAT PAPERWORK REALLY ISN'T THAT IMPORTANT.
LET'S MOVE ON TO YOUR ADDRESS, CONTACT INFORMATION...
YOU DON'T NEED TO SEE THAT EITHER.
DO YOU?
YOU KNOW WHAT? I TOTALLY DON'T!

energy drink
energy drink
energy drink
WHAT ARE YOU LOOKING FOR HERE... EXACTLY?
INTELLIGENCE ANALYSIS IS OUR M.O.S.
THAT'S "MILITARY OCCUPATIONAL SPECIALTY."
'ROID RAGERS
EACH HUMAN BEING HAS TWENTY-THREE CHROMOSOME PAIRS.
THAT'S APPROXIMATELY 8.3 MILLION COMBINATIONS.
BUT IN A PLANET WITH 7.3 BILLION PEOPLE ON IT...
...THAT MEANS 1-IN-880 PEOPLE ARE, BASICALLY, THE SAME.
EVERY SCHOOL WE GO TO, EVERYWHERE, HAS THE SAME CLIQUES BREAKING DOWN THE SAME PHYSICAL, INTELLECTUAL AND CLASS LINES.
SO EACH SCHOOL VISIT IS LIKE CODEBREAKING.
DRAMA QUEENS

WE ARE LOOKING FOR "CLUES."
NOT PHYSICAL CLUES, MIND YOU, BUT BEHAVIORAL AND SOCIAL PATTERNS WORTHY OF ADDITIONAL SCRUTINY.
UH... WHAT?
KEYS CLUB
CYBERGEEKS
OUTLIERS
WE ELIMINATE REDUNDANCIES, REDUCING THE DATA STRINGS TO THEIR SMALLEST POSSIBLE TRANSLATABLE UNIT.
AND IT IS FROM THESE ANOMALIES WE WILL DISCOVER THE MOST PROMISING AVENUES OF ATTACK.
HUH.
AND HERE I THOUGHT I WAS SO UNIQUE.
WE KNOW.

GUYS, PEOPLE ARE STARING. IS THE HOLDING HANDS... UH...
...REALLY NECESSARY?
NOT IN THE LEAST.
BUT WE FIND IT COMFORTING.
LIGHTS TOO LOUD... SOOOO HUNGOVER...
ADELE!
THANKS AGAIN FOR INVITING ME TO THE PARTY LAST NIGHT...
MOMOO
HOPE YOU ENJOYED IT, NARC, BECAUSE IT'S NOT A MISTAKE I'LL MAKE TWICE.
UH... WHAT?
THERE'S A REASON NON-MEMBERS DON'T GET INVITED TO KEYS CLUB PARTIES! IN A MOMENT OF WEAKNESS I FELT SORRY FOR YOU--
--BUT YOU HAD YOUR DAD COME BUST US! IF THAT ENDS UP ON MY PERMANENT TRANSCRIPTS, YOUR ASS IS MINE, SHERMAN!
BUT--I DIDN'T DO ANYTHING! I DIDN'T TELL ANYBODY!
MAYBE IF YOU SPOILED BRATS DIDN'T BLARE MUSIC SO THE NEXT COUNTY COULD HEAR THE SHERIFF WOULDN'T HAVE BEEN CALLED!
DROP DEAD, KEISHA!
HMM.
TAKE US TO HER LOCKER.

PRETTY SURE THIS IS IT, BUT YOU'RE NOT GETTING IN THERE WITHOUT HER STUDENT ID.

YOU DON'T SAY.

WHOA. ***LARCENOUS!***

BWEEEP

AS WE SUSPECTED.

WHAT?

HAS ANYONE EVER TOLD YOU YOU SAY "WHAT" A LOT?

AND DID YOU KNOW THAT ADELE POOLE, CAPTAIN OF THE CHEERLEADING SQUAD, PRESIDENT OF THE KEYS CLUB...

...HAS SOMETHING OF A ***FIXATION*** ON YOUR DECEASED BOYFRIEND?

WHA... WHA...

WHAT DO YOU THINK YOU'RE *DOING,* POKING AROUND MY GIRLFRIEND'S LOCKER?
COULD YOU PLEASE CLARIFY TO WHICH LOCKER YOU ARE REFERRING?
DON'T GET SMART WITH ME!
WE WOULD NOT DREAM OF GETTING SMART WITH YOU.
IF WE DID GET SMART WITH YOU, YOU WOULD START BLEEDING FROM YOUR EARS.
WHAT?
HMH. IT'S CONTAGIOUS.
YOUR EXCEPTIONALLY MEASURED HEARTBEAT. IT LETS YOU EXCEL AT THE SPORTSBALL, DRAKE MATHESON.
WHA... HOW'D YOU KNOW MY--?

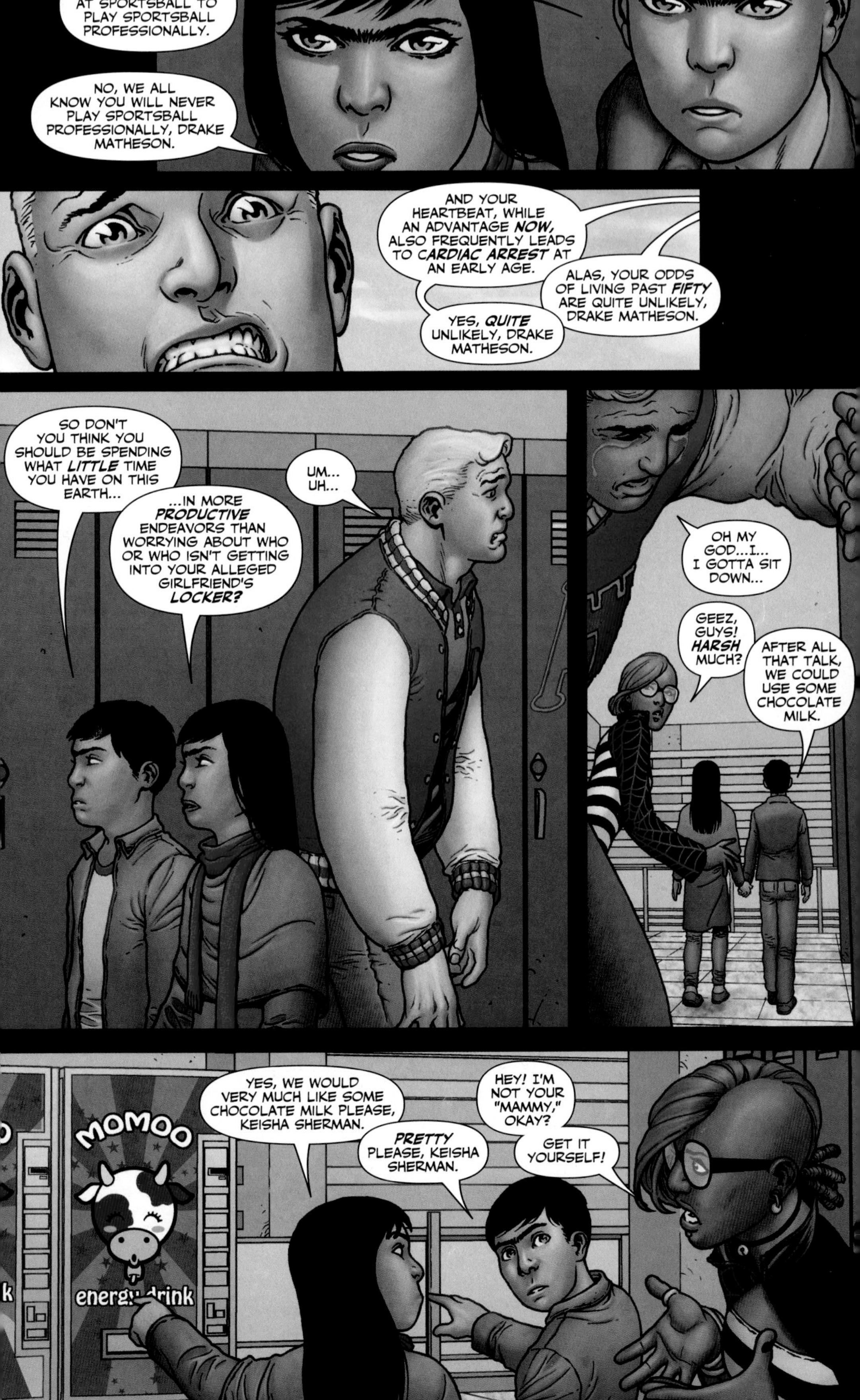
AT SPORTSBALL TO PLAY SPORTSBALL PROFESSIONALLY.
NO, WE ALL KNOW YOU WILL NEVER PLAY SPORTSBALL PROFESSIONALLY, DRAKE MATHESON.
AND YOUR HEARTBEAT, WHILE AN ADVANTAGE NOW, ALSO FREQUENTLY LEADS TO CARDIAC ARREST AT AN EARLY AGE.
YES, QUITE UNLIKELY, DRAKE MATHESON.
ALAS, YOUR ODDS OF LIVING PAST FIFTY ARE QUITE UNLIKELY, DRAKE MATHESON.
SO DON'T YOU THINK YOU SHOULD BE SPENDING WHAT LITTLE TIME YOU HAVE ON THIS EARTH...
...IN MORE PRODUCTIVE ENDEAVORS THAN WORRYING ABOUT WHO OR WHO ISN'T GETTING INTO YOUR ALLEGED GIRLFRIEND'S LOCKER?
UM... UH...
OH MY GOD...I... I GOTTA SIT DOWN...
GEEZ, GUYS! HARSH MUCH?
AFTER ALL THAT TALK, WE COULD USE SOME CHOCOLATE MILK.
MOMOO
energy drink
YES, WE WOULD VERY MUCH LIKE SOME CHOCOLATE MILK PLEASE, KEISHA SHERMAN.
PRETTY PLEASE, KEISHA SHERMAN.
HEY! I'M NOT YOUR "MAMMY," OKAY?
GET IT YOURSELF!

NEVER EVER EVER DRINKING AGAIN...
NOT UNTIL I GET INTO HARVARD...
HEY.
WHAT DO YOU THINK YOU'RE LOOKING AT, COWGIRL?
NOT MUCH.

DO YOU KNOW WHO I AM?
WOULD BE SOMEWHERE ELSE IF I DIDN'T.
I'M GONNA COUNT TO FIVE, PERV.
AND YOU'D BETTER BE SOMEWHERE ELSE.
THAT'S RIGHT.
IS THAT RIGHT?
DON'T LET HER CLEAR FOUR, ANIMALIA.
"ANIMALIA?"
WHAT IS THAT?
SOME KINDA TOWNIE DRUG SLANG?

LOOKOUT PARK.
UH...YOU GUYS...
...IS HIDING OUT IN THE FIREWATCH TOWER REALLY THE SMARTEST WAY TO STAY UNDER-THE-RADAR?
I MEAN IT IS THE TALLEST BUILDING IN TOWN...
MICHIGAN
ZHM 619
GREAT LAKE STATE
WE FOLLOW ORDERS, KEISHA SHERMAN.
AND THIS IS WHERE COMMANDER CRONUS HAS CHOSEN TO ESTABLISH HIS F.O.B.
KEISHA! KEISHA SHERMAN!
SO GOOD TO FINALLY MEET YOU IN THE FLESH!
NGGGGK!
YOU HAVE THE MOST BEAUTIFUL THOUGHTS. THEY'RE ALL SHINY AND SMOOTH AND PERFECTLY FORMED-- LIKE RIVER STONES.
UH... THANKS?
AND YOUR NAME--
MY NAME IS CLOUD.
AND YOU'RE THE ONE--
I AM THE ONE WHO CAN READ MINDS, YES.
UH-HUH. CHECKS OUT.

TEEHEE! KEISHA SHERMAN IS FUNNY.
KEISHA SHERMAN DRESSES TOUGH-GOTH TO MAKE PEOPLE THINK SHE HATES THEM BUT REALLY SHE FEELS TOO MUCH AND IT'S HARD TO LET THEM GET CLOSE LIKE YOUR BARE HAND ON A FURNACE.
SMEK
KEISHA SHERMAN GETS VERY QUIET AROUND THE TRUTH.
KEISHA SHERMAN IS A GOOD PERSON.
KEISHA SHERMAN DID NOT KILL STEPHEN SEO. IT WAS NOT HER FAULT.
...
NO MATTER HOW MUCH KEISHA SHERMAN THINKS OTHERWISE.
WE ARE GOING TO BE BESTEST FRIENDS, KEISHA SHERMAN!
WHOA.
YEAH.
CLOUD DOESN'T JUST READ INDIVIDUAL MINDS--SHE'S EXPOSED, ALL THE TIME, TO HUMANITY'S COLLECTIVE CONSCIOUSNESS.
SHE HEARS EVERYBODY, ALWAYS. THE INSIDE OF HER HEAD IS ONE INFINITE YOUTUBE COMMENTS PAGE.
OUCH. THAT EXPLAINS WHY SHE'S SO...
CLOUD IS MADE OF LIGHT, KEISHA. SHE CHOOSES TO BE MADE OF LIGHT.
SHE IS HER OWN BEST COUNTER AGAINST THE DARKNESS.

SO SHE'LL NEED YOUR HELP IN INTERROGATING OUR PRIME SUSPECT.
AND THAT WOULD BE...?
SHERMAN!
I KNEW YOU WERE BEHIND THIS! I TRY TO BE NICE TO YOU EVEN THOUGH YOU'RE A HUGE LOSER-- AND THIS IS THE THANKS I GET!
YOU BETTER HOPE YOUR JUVIE FREAK FRIENDS KILL ME--
--BECAUSE IF THEY DON'T, I SWEAR TO DOLCE AND GABANA--
--YOUR DADDY WON'T BE ABLE TO SAVE YOU, GOD IN HEAVEN WON'T BE ABLE TO SAVE YOU--
--BECAUSE YOU ARE DEAD, YOU HEAR ME, SHERMAN?
DEAD!
THIS DAY JUST KEEPS GETTING BETTER AND BETTER.

GENERATION ZERO™

WE ARE THE FUTURE.

THOSE *LOSERS* PRANKED ME--

ON PROM NIGHT?!

CHEESE IT!

Adele IN: THESE KIDS TODAY!
KEYS CLUB BAKE SALE! RAISING MONEY FOR THE SURVIVORS OF MEXICO CITY!
C'MON, ROOK HIGH! HAVE A HEART...
...AND A BROWNIE!
BAKE SALE!
OOH! OOH!
ME!
SIGH!
GIMME AN R! GIMME AN O! GIMME ANOTHER O--
PANT PANT GIMME A BREAK!

...AND IN CONCLUSION, I HAVE INCONTROVERTIBLY PROVEN GLOBAL WARMING IS NOT A HOAX!
BATE TEAM
GASP! SHE'S DONE IT!

MISS! MISS?
CAN I HAVE ONE EXTREMELY SMALL FREE CUP OF WATER, PLEASE?
WIENER QUEEN
MISS? CAN YOU HEAR ME?
JUST A SECOND PUFF! SIR! WE'RE A LITTLE PUFF! SHORT HANDED- TODAY!

TSK! SLEEPING UNTIL TEN A.M.--ON A SATURDAY!
HARVARD, HERE I COME!
ZZZZADVANCED PLACEMENTZZZZ
MOMOO

SWEET EXTRA CREDIT!
BRAAAAAA

WHA'--WHA' HAPPENED?!
TEENAGERS TODAY--SO LAZY!
Y'KNOW...

.HANGING OUT WITH YOU GUYS MAKES ME EEL LIKE I WASTED MY WHOLE LIFE NOT DOING DRUGS FOR NOTHING.
WHAT THE HELL IS GOING ON HERE?
FOLLOW UP QUESTION:
WHY DO I LOOK LIKE A CARTOON?
WE'RE INSIDE ADELE POOLE'S MIND, KEISHA.
WITH RESPECT, COMMANDER CRONUS, THAT'S NOT QUITE ACCURATE.
"RATHER, OUR OPERATIONAL CONSCIOUSNESS IS INSIDE ADELE'S CONSCIOUSNESS...
"...WHO WE SORTA KIDNAPPED...
"...WHILE OUR PHYSICAL BODIES REMAIN IN THE LOOKOUT PARK TOWER...
"...THANKS TO GAMETE THE SUPER-FETUS, WHO CAN PSYCHICALLY SWAP CONSCIOUSNESSES, JUST AS SHE POSSESSES HER COMATOSE MOTHER."
CASTLES

SO...WE'RE INSIDE HER MIND.
THAT'S WHAT HE SAID.
SIGH NO, KEISHA.
COULD YOU PLEASE STOP BEING SO DISTRESSINGLY NORMAL FOR ONCE IN YOUR LIFE?

UNTIL I MET YOU GUYS, MOST PEOPLE THOUGHT I WAS PRETTY WEIRD, ACTUALLY.
HAVE YOU NOT SEEN MY HAIR--?!

ALL OF OUR CONSCIOUSNESSES ARE A CONTINUUM OF MEMORIES, BELIEF SYSTEMS, PERCEPTIONS OF THE PRESENT, DESIRES FOR THE FUTURE, ET CETERA.
ULTIMATELY, HOWEVER, WE ALL BELIEVE WE ARE THE HEROES OF OUR OWN NARRATIVE.
...

COMMANDER CRONUS, FOR EXAMPLE, SEES HIMSELF AS A REVOLUTIONARY.
"SEES HIMSELF?" HEY!

WHILE YOU SEE YOURSELF AS THE DEMURE, GOTH-Y TYPE.
LIFE.
I CANNOT BEAR IT, YET I CANNOT THROW IT AWAY...

THIS IS HOW ADELE POOLE SEES HERSELF.
THIS IS HER "HEROSCAPE."
AND IN IT WE SHOULD BE ABLE TO LEARN THINGS THAT SHE WOULD NOT, OR COULD NOT, TELL US CONSCIOUSLY.

WAIT...AND NONE OF YOU HAVE AN ETHICAL ISSUE WITH THIS?
DEFINE ETHICS?
OKAY, ANIMALIA, WE NEED YOU TO *RECON* THIS HEROSCAPE AS QUICKLY AS YOU CAN.
SIR YES, SIR!

SINCE *EVERYTHING* AROUND US LOOKS LIKE BABY STUFF, I DON'T MIND TURNING *INTO* BABY STUFF FOR ONCE!
WHATEVER GETS YOU TO FOLLOW ORDERS, I'M ALL FOR.

WHAT *IS* THE ETHICAL ISSUE, EXACTLY?
SHE COULD HAVE INFORMATION VITAL TO OUR INVESTIGATION INTO *YOUR* BOYFRIEND'S DEATH, AND WE ARE EXTRACTING THAT INFORMATION WITHOUT HARMING HER PHYSICALLY.

BUT BY SCOOPING IT OUT OF HER MOST PRIVATE SPACES-- INVOLUNTARILY!
SHE'S THE *ENEMY,* KEISHA. A PRISONER OF WAR--
WHAT WAR? WHOSE WAR? SHE'S NOT "THE ENEMY," SHE'S A *HIGH SCHOOL SENIOR--*
THAT DOESN'T MAKE HER INNOCENT.

THAT DOESN'T MEAN WE NEED TO TREAT HER LIKE *BIN LADEN,* EITHER!
NOT EVERYTHING REQUIRES A MILITARY SOLUTION!
AGREE TO DISAGREE. IF WE HAD MORE *MILITARY SOLUTIONS,* THE WORLD WOULD BE A MORE *PEACEFUL* PLACE.
THAT... MAKES *NO SENSE,* YOU REALIZE?

WHY DON'T WE SEE WHAT ELSE ADELE'S HEROSCAPE HAS TO OFFER BEFORE YOU JUMP TO ANY CONCLUSIONS?
HEY! THE WIENER QUEEN! THAT'S WHERE I WORK, TOO!
I REMEMBER THIS DAY!

Adele in: Skank Attack!

WOW, YOUR DAD MADE YOU GET A JOB AT WIENER QUEEN EVEN THOUGH HE'S THE EMERGENCY MANAGER OF THE WHOLE DARN TOWN, HUH?

HE MADE THE EXCELLENT POINT THAT LOWERING MYSELF TO THE LEVEL OF THE COMMON FOLK WILL MAKE ME MORE RELATABLE TO HARVARD ADMISSIONS!

WOW, YOU'RE GONNA BE OUR NEXT FEMALE PRESIDENT, ADELE POOLE!

WIENER QUEEN

YOUR SIGHTS ARE TOO *LOW*, DRAKE DARLING!

I'M GOING TO BE THE NEXT FEMALE PRESIDENT WITH AN ACADEMY AWARD AND A GRAMMY!
HEY! HEY! ADELE! YOU FORGOT--

--YOU FORGOT TO TAKE MY ORDER!

...I LOVE YOU.

I HAD NO IDEA...
I MEAN, STEPHEN TOLD ME HE AND ADELE HAD MADE OUT WHILE THEY WERE IN THE *KEYS CLUB* TOGETHER, I DIDN'T THINK THEY WERE ACTUALLY *DATING...*

THEY PROBABLY *WEREN'T.*
DON'T FORGET THIS IS HOW *ADELE* SEES HER WORLD, NOT HOW HER WORLD ACTUALLY *IS.*
SHE SEES HERSELF...AS THIS PUT-UPON UNDERDOG? SHE'S THE MOST POPULAR GIRL IN SCHOOL--I DON'T KNOW ANYONE WHO ISN'T IN *AWE* OF HER!
THAT'S BECAUSE THEY NEVER SEE THE WORLD THROUGH *HER* EYES, I GUESS...

HEY YOU GUYS!
DID YOU HEAR SOMETHING?
UP HERE.
WAIT, NO, LET ME GUESS:
YOU'RE *CLOUD.*

TEE HEE!
YOU'RE SO FUNNY AND *SMART,* KEISHA SHERMAN!
AND *PRETTY,* TOO!
...THANKS.

CRONUS, I NEED TO UPDATE THE SIT-REP.
GO HEAD, COMM SPECIALIST.
OUR LITTLE FRIEND ADELE IS A WEEEEE BIT SNEAKIER THAN WE THOUGHT!
HER LONG-TERM MEMORIES AND "HEROSCAPE" ARE JUST CHOCK TO THE BRIM WITH MILITARY-GRADE PSYCHIC SAFE-GUARDS!
MILITARY--? LIKE...WHAT? HARBINGER FOUNDATION? PROJECT RISING SPIRIT?
A BIG TEE-BEE-DEE ON THAT ONE, CRONUS!
GAMETE DETECTED THE ANTIBODIES--AND THEY'VE DETECTED YOU. THEY'LL LOBOTOMIZE YOU AS SOON AS YOU TRY TO REMOVE YOURSELVES FROM ADELE'S MIND!
AGAIN, "MIND" IS AN UNQUANTIFIABLE ABSTRACT. THE MORE ACCURATE--
GIVE IT A REST, LIEUTENANT. WRAP IT UP, CLOUD.
I'M AFRAID YOU'RE GOING TO HAVE TO STAY PUT IN THERE UNTIL GAMETE AND I NOODLE OUT AN EXIT STRATEGY!
WAIT, WHAT?! BUT I'M SUPPOSED TO MAKE DINNER FOR MY BROTHER!
WHO'S GONNA BE THERE WHEN KWAME GETS HOME FROM SCHOOL? WHO--
MISSION REDIRECT, TELIC-- STAY ALIVE UNTIL WE CAN BE EXTRACTED.
COPY THAT.
BUT THEY MAY HAVE SOMETHING TO SAY ABOUT IT, COMMANDER.

OH NO! CORNERMEN!
BAWL LACONIC! PUNK!
CLOUD-- FIND ANIMALIA-- TELL HER WE NEED AIR SUPPORT!
ON IT.
LADIES--THIS HAS TURNED INTO A REARGUARD ACTION!
A WHAT--WHAT WHAT?
I DON'T SPEAK YOUR CRAZY MOON LANGUAGE!!

IT MEANS RUN!
THEN WHY NOT JUST SAY "RUN"?!
IT'S LESS SYLLABLES!
EVEN WITH AN ARMY OF THESE THINGS, THEY'RE STILL BASICALLY JUST HAZMAT SUITS WITH ATTITUDE, WE SHOULD MAKE EASY WORK OF--
BAP
AW, CRAP.
ICY TERN.
KRRRRRRRRKK
COMMANDER--IN "HEROSCAPE"--THE CORNERMEN--
--ARE VIRTUALLY INVINCIBLE!
I NOTICED, I NOTICED!

GUYS! GUYS!
OVER HERE!
THE CORNERMEN NEED RIGHT ANGLES TO TELEPORT THROUGH, RIGHT?
AND THE ROLLER RINK IS COMPLETELY ROUND!
WE COULD TAKE SHELTER... IN...UH...
Eep!
WHAT DO YOU THINK?
ABSOLUTELY NOT.
GOT ANY BETTER IDEAS?
LET'S MOTOR.

Adele IN: OH GOD WHY WON'T YOU JUST LET ME DIE?

BABY? BABY, WON'T YOU...
C'MON, ADELE, I WISH YOU'D LET ME IN...
RATTLE RATTLE RATTLE
NO! GO AWAY, DAD!
I'M WORRIED ABOUT YOU, BUTTERCUP.
IF YOU DON'T WANT TO TALK TO ME, AT LEAST COME OUT AND TALK TO SOMEBODY. YOUR FRIENDS--THE KEYS CLUB--
NO! STEPHEN IS DEAD AND YOU DON'T CARE!
I LOVED HIM AND YOU DIDN'T DO ANYTHING TO STOP IT!
I KNOW... I KNOW YOU MAY FIND THIS HARD TO BELIEVE, ADELE, BUT THERE'S ONLY SO MUCH I CAN DO.
THE ONLY PERSON TO BLAME FOR STEPHEN'S DEATH IS STEPHEN.
NOW WE CAN'T HAVE YOU STAY IN YOUR ROOM ALL WEEKEND.
WHAT WOULD HARVARD ADMISSIONS SAY?
MON

OH--
OH NO! I-IT'S LOCKED--
DEED TEETHING NOSTRIL!
GAS MAIN. THERE.
COPY.
TRYING ALL POSSIBLE COMBOS NOW....
NO.
NO.
YES.
NO.
NO.
NO.
NO.
YES.
NO.
NO.
KLIK
YES!

HOW CAN YOU DO STUFF LIKE THAT?!
YOU WOULDN'T UNDERSTAND IF I TOLD YOU.
C'MON, I'M NOT AN IDIOT.
WELL, MY MIND HAS BEEN ACCELERATED INTO THE QUANTUM STREAM.
I CAN BOTH SEE A FEW SECONDS INTO THE FUTURE AND MOVE IN AND OUT OF LOCALIZED TEMPORAL STATES.
PSSH!
I MEAN, YEAH, DUH, OBVIOUSLY.
CLOUD! DO YOU COPY, CLOUD?
OUR EZ IS RED HOT!
THIS IS A ROUND BUILDING, SO THERE'S NO CORNERS FOR THE ENEMY TO TELEPORT IN FROM--
--BUT THEY'RE TRYING AS HARD AS THEY CAN TO GET IN THE TRADITIONAL WAY!
WE NEED EXTRACTION NOW!

SLIIIIIIGHT PROBLEM WITH THAT, COMMANDER ...
NO TIME FOR EXCUSES, CLOUD!
GAMETE FIGURED OUT WE CAN SAFELY PULL YOU OUT THROUGH EACH OTHER'S CONSCIOUS-NESSES, FOOLING ADELE'S DEFENSES...
...EXCEPT THERE'S A RESISTANCE HERE...YOU'RE ALL NETWORKED TOGETHER...AND ONE OF YOU ISN'T COMPLYING WITH THE DEPARTURE...
...TRAPPING YOU ALL IN THERE!
WHO IS IT?!
DON'T LOOK AT ME! I DIDN'T WANT TO COME HERE IN THE FIRST PLACE!
MAKES TWO OF US.
WHO...?
OH, I KNOW.
I KNOW.
ANIMALIA? IS THAT YOU, KIDDO?
DON'T
SNIFF
DON'T CALL ME KIDDO.
I'M GETTING MORE GROWN UP EVERY DAY.
I DON'T EVEN WANT TO TURN INTO THIS BABY STUFF ANYMORE.

SSHKKKSSSSHHH
YOU WON'T TURN INTO ANYTHING EVER AGAIN IF YOU DON'T LEAVE WITH US, HONEY.
BUT--I'VE BEEN ALL AROUND THIS PLACE, COMMANDER--AND IT'S SO NICE.
EVERYONE IS SO NICE.
I MEAN, SURE THEY HAVE PROBLEMS, BUT THEY'RE ALL TEMPORARY AND AFTER EVERYONE HAS A LAUGH THEY'RE JUST BACK TO THE WAY THEY WERE BEFORE!
BUT-- KIDDO--
STOP CALLING ME KIDDO IF YOU'RE NOT GONNA LET ME BE A KID!
ALL WE DO IS FIGHT! I'M SO SICK OF IT! WE FIGHT AND FIGHT AND FIGHT AND NOTHING EVER CHANGES!
I DON'T WANT TO DO WAR ANYMORE! I WANNA STAY HERE!
YOU LITTLE BRAT! YOU'RE GONNA GET US ALL KILLED!
GEEZ, CHILL OUT, OKAY? SHE IS JUST A KID...
ANIMALIA, THIS "HEROSCAPE"... IT'S NOT REAL, YOU KNOW?
I KNOW IT SEEMS NICE, BUT THAT'S A WAY ADELE CAN HIDE FROM HER REAL PROBLEMS.

WHAT WE'VE GOTTA DO, IS MAKE A PLACE LIKE THIS... BUT OUT THERE.
OUT THERE IS THE REAL WORLD. THE REAL WORLD SUCKS.
YEAH... IT DOES, SOMETIMES.
BUT WE WOULDN'T HAVE THIS WORLD WITHOUT IT.
AND IF WE DON'T GO PROTECT THE REAL ONE--THIS ONE WILL GO WITH IT, YOU KNOW?
AND I PROMISE, ANIMALIA-- MONICA.
GENERATION ZERO ONLY FIGHTS SO WE CAN STOP FIGHTING, ONE DAY.
AND I THINK THAT IN ROOK WE MAY HAVE FINALLY FOUND THE HOME WE NEED.
YEAH. YOU SEE?
ONCE WE TAKE IT OVER, THAT IS.
WAIT.
WHAT?
THIS IS ALL VERY TOUCHING, NO REALLY, I'M MOVED BEYOND WORDS!
CLOUD WE NEED TO BE PULLED OUTTA HERE RIGHT! NOW!

EASY-PEASY, LEMON-SQUEASY!

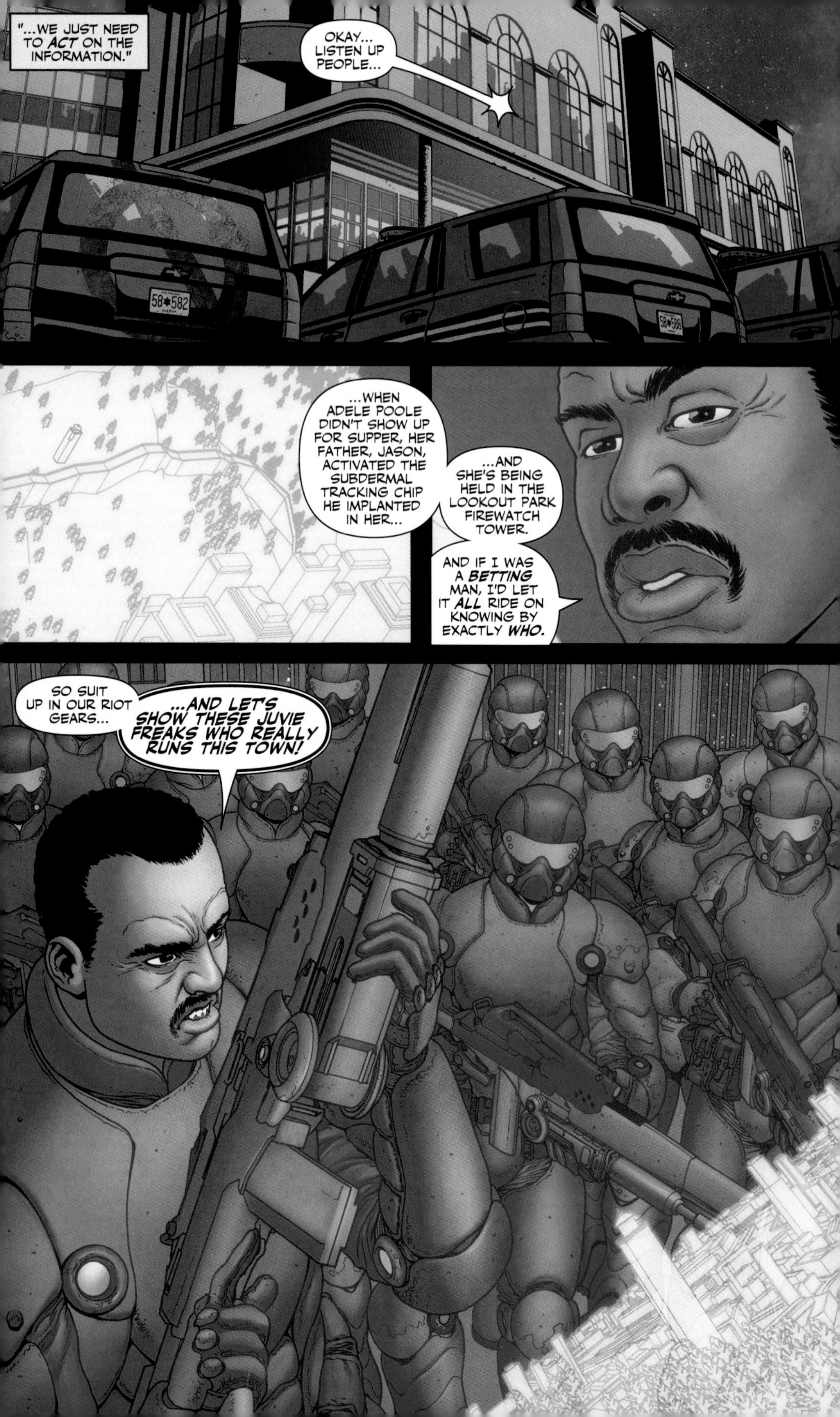

"...WE JUST NEED TO *ACT* ON THE INFORMATION."

OKAY... LISTEN UP PEOPLE...

...WHEN ADELE POOLE DIDN'T SHOW UP FOR SUPPER, HER FATHER, JASON, ACTIVATED THE SUBDERMAL TRACKING CHIP HE IMPLANTED IN HER...

...AND SHE'S BEING HELD IN THE LOOKOUT PARK FIREWATCH TOWER.

AND IF I WAS A *BETTING* MAN, I'D LET IT *ALL* RIDE ON KNOWING BY EXACTLY *WHO.*

SO SUIT UP IN OUR RIOT GEARS...

...AND LET'S SHOW THESE JUVIE FREAKS WHO REALLY RUNS THIS TOWN!

VALIANT | FRED VAN LENTE | FRANCIS PORTELA
ANDREW DALHOUSE

GENERATION ZERO

ER ROOM
ULES

SHERIFF

ROOK SPECIAL EDUCATION SCHOOL, LAZARUS LANE SE.

KEISHA! THANK GOD, I WAS REALLY STARTING TO WORRY--

YEAH, I'M SORRY, MS. OOSTING, BUT I'M NOT GONNA BE ABLE TO MAKE IT TO PICK UP MY BROTHER--

FIREWATCH TOWER, LOOKOUT PARK.

--DON'T WORRY, I'M GONNA CALL MY DAD RIGHT NOW, I'M SURE HE'LL COME OVER--OR SEND ONE OF HIS DEPUTIES OVER AS SOON AS HE CAN--

THE SHERIFF? OKAY, THANKS, I'LL LET HIM KNOW RIGHT NOW.

KWAME? THAT WAS YOUR SISTER. SHE CAN'T MAKE IT, SO YOUR DAD'S GONNA SEND SOMEBODY TO COME GET YOU.
BUT KEISHA ALWAYS GETS ME.
KEISHA ALWAYS GETS ME AT--
RIGHT. BUT REMEMBER WE'VE DISCUSSED THIS? SOMETIMES THINGS HAPPEN. THE UNEXPECTED HAPPENS. THIS IS ONE OF THOSE TIMES--
SEE? THERE'S THE SHERIFF NOW.
I'VE GOT TO HELP PERCY FIND HIS BUS, SO I'LL SEE YOU TOMORROW, OKAY?

A KIDNAPPING? FIRST EXCITEMENT WE'VE HAD AROUND HERE SINCE THAT KOREAN KID WRAPPED HIS ASS AROUND A TREE.
THINK SHERMAN WILL FINALLY LET US BREAK OUT THE *RRRRIOT GEARS?*
HE'D BETTER. THEY'RE LIKE A BOX SITTING UNDER THE TREE ON CHRISTMAS EVE.
JUST BEGGING US TO UNWRAP IT.
WOOWOOWOOWOO
WOOWOOWOOWOO
SKRREEEEEEEEEEEEEEECH
GOOD.
THEY'RE GONE.
IT'S *KEISHA* WHO ALWAYS GETS ME.

--SO I CAN'T PICK UP WAME TODAY, DAD. ALLY SORRY ABOUT HAT, BUT THIS TRIG TEST IS SUPER-IMPORTANT.
PLEASE CALL ME AS SOON AS YOU GET THIS MESSAGE SO I KNOW YOU WERE ABLE TO GET HIM, OKAY? THANKS! LOVE YOU!
I'D RATHER YOU'D *DIDN'T* COME WITH US, KEISHA.
ARE YOU HIGH? I *STARTED* THIS INVESTIGATION, I'M GONNA SEE IT ALL THE WAY THROUGH, NO MATTER WHERE IT TAKES ME.
BESIDES, I'M ESSENTIAL!
I'VE GOT THE CAR!
I... JUST.
WE'RE HERE TO HELP KIDS.
AND THIS IS THE FIRST TIME WE MAY BE IN REAL DANGER.
I DON'T WANT...
I DON'T WANT YOU TO BE HURT.
THANKS, BUT I CAN TAKE CARE OF MYSELF.
AGAINST NORMAL PEOPLE, SURE.
I'M NOT NORMAL!
WHY DOES EVERYONE KEEP *SAYING* THAT?!
I WISH YOU WOULDN'T COME EITHER.

DIDN'T KNOW YOU CARED, TELIC.
I DON'T.
BUT YOU'RE A DISTRACTION TO HIM.
WE WERE RAISED TO BE HUMAN WEAPONS, SHERMAN--
--NO, NOT EVEN WEAPONS. PROJECTILES.
TO BE AIMED AND FIRED AT NAMELESS BATTLEFIELDS. TO KILL AND DIE UNKNOWN AND UNLOVED.
"THEN HE CAME ALONG. CRONUS.
"HE FREED US--NOT JUST OUR BODIES. OUR MINDS.
"AND GAVE US SOMETHING TO FIGHT FOR."
A PLACE OF OUR OWN.
JESUS. JEALOUS MUCH?
I'M STILL NOT OVER MY BOYFRIEND, I DON'T HAVE DESIGNS ON YOURS--

HEY--
NFFF! HEY! QUIT IT!
YOU DON'T GET IT.

YOU ARE A CHILD. YOU THINK LIKE A CHILD. YOUR UNDERSTANDING OF THE WORLD, IS A CHILD'S.
THAT'S NOT--
WE NEVER HAD THAT.

DO YOU UNDERSTAND? DO YOU UNDERSTAND HOW MUCH I ENVY YOU?
BUT THAT LONG, BLOODY SCREAM WHERE OUR CHILDHOODS SHOULD BE--
--THAT'S THE ONLY REASON WE'RE STILL ALIVE.

IF I CATCH YOU DISTRACTING CRONUS--WEAKENING HIM--WITH YOUR, YOUR, I DON'T KNOW WHAT CALL IT--
--YOUR MILITANT INNOCENCE--
--KNOW ONE THING, SHERMAN:

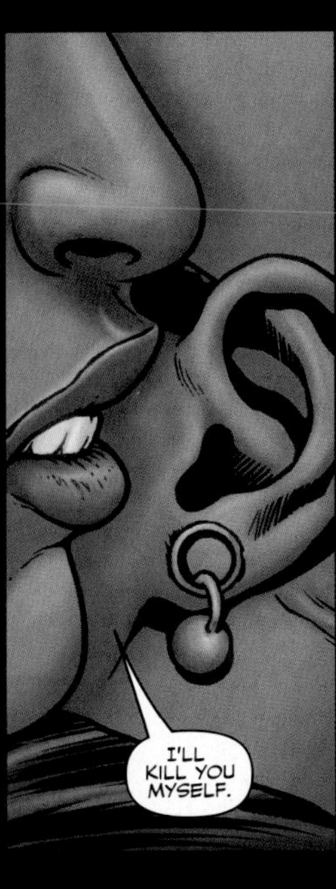
I'LL KILL YOU MYSELF.

IT'S NOT FAIR.
YOU HAVE POWERS AND THAT'S ALL YOU HAVE.
NO CONSCIENCE. NO RESPONSIBILITY. NOTHING TO LOSE.
GRRRRRRRRRRRR
CASTLES
YOU DON'T CARE WHO YOU HURT, BECAUSE YOU DON'T KNOW WHAT IT'S LIKE TO BUILD SOMETHING.
WHATEVER YOU DO IS JUSTIFIED. YOUR WHOLE LIVES ARE ONE LONG, ACT OF REVENGE.
WHAT YOU'RE TALKING ABOUT IS SOMETHING NIETZSCHE CALLED "MASTER-SLAVE MORALITY."
THE WEAK DEFINE THE STRONG AS EVIL, FOR BEING STRONG AND OPPRESSING THEM.
AND THE STRONG DEFINE THE WEAK AS EVIL, FOR BEING WEAK...
NIETZSCHE.
WHAT?
...AND FOR ALLOWING THEMSELVES TO BE OPPRESSED.
BEYOND GOOD AND EVIL. YOU SHOULD CHECK IT OUT.

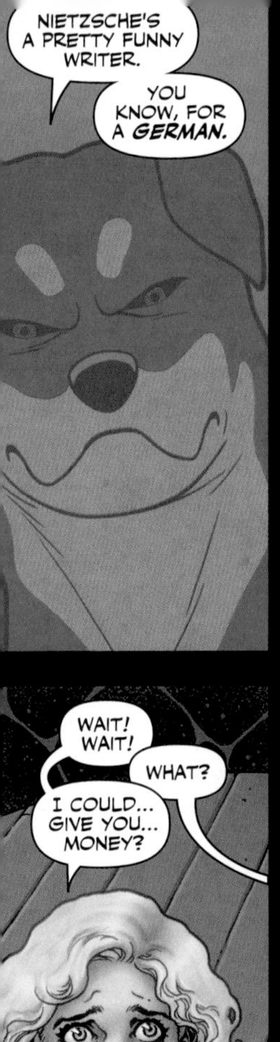
NIETZSCHE'S A PRETTY FUNNY WRITER.
YOU KNOW, FOR A **GERMAN.**

IT WAS REQUIRED READING AS PART OF OUR ***ETHICS TRAINING*** IN THE ***NURSERY.***

THE NURSERY? WHAT WAS THAT?
WERE YOU FREAKS GROWN IN ***TUBES*** OR SOMETHING?
OR STITCHED TOGETHER FROM THE CORPSES OF THE KIDS YOU'VE MURDERED?
CASTLES

Heh.
YOU'RE CUTE.

WAIT! WAIT!
WHAT?
I COULD... GIVE YOU... MONEY?
CASTLES

DO I LOOK ***DRIVEN*** BY A ***PROFIT MOTIVE*** TO YOU?

THEN--YOU SHOULD SEE THE TECHNOLOGY MY DAD HAS ACCESS TO IN THIS TOWN!
CASTLES

POSSESSIONS ARE A BURDEN.
ALSO: THEY ARE ***LAME.***

THEN--
CASTLES

THEN TAKE ME WITH YOU!
CASTLES

...

WHAT?

I WANT TO HELP.
I WANT...
I WANT TO *MEAN* SOMETHING.
PLEASE.
DO ME A FAVOR, ADELE.
DON'T EVER CHANGE.
MMMMMF!

TELIC.
I DO NOT LIKE TO ENTER YOUR THOUGHTS BECAUSE THEY ARE A SEETHING QUANTUM STORM OF MEMORIES THAT NEVER HAPPENED AND REGRETS OF THINGS YOU HAVEN'T YET DONE.
SO I AM TELLING YOU WITH MY CLUMSY MOUTH-SPEAK, WITH THE SPIT AND THE TONGUE AND THE INFLECTION OF THE DIAPHRAGM:
THE COMMANDER SAYS IT IS TIME TO DEPLOY.
HOOAH.
YES.
WHAT?
WHAT YOU'RE THINKING?
NO, IT'S NOT JUST YOU.
YES, SHE IS ALWAYS LIKE THAT.

LET'S GO, ANIMALIA, COME ON!
HONK HONK
YOU TAKE CARE OF ADELE?
AYUP.
OH MY GOD YOU DIDN'T KILL HER, DID YOU?!
OF COURSE NOT! GEEZ, KEISHA, WHEN WILL YOU GET IT THROUGH YOUR HEAD WE'RE NOT MONSTERS.
YOU... DIDN'T KILL HER, RIGHT?
NO.
WAIT. WAS I SUPPOSED TO?
NO!

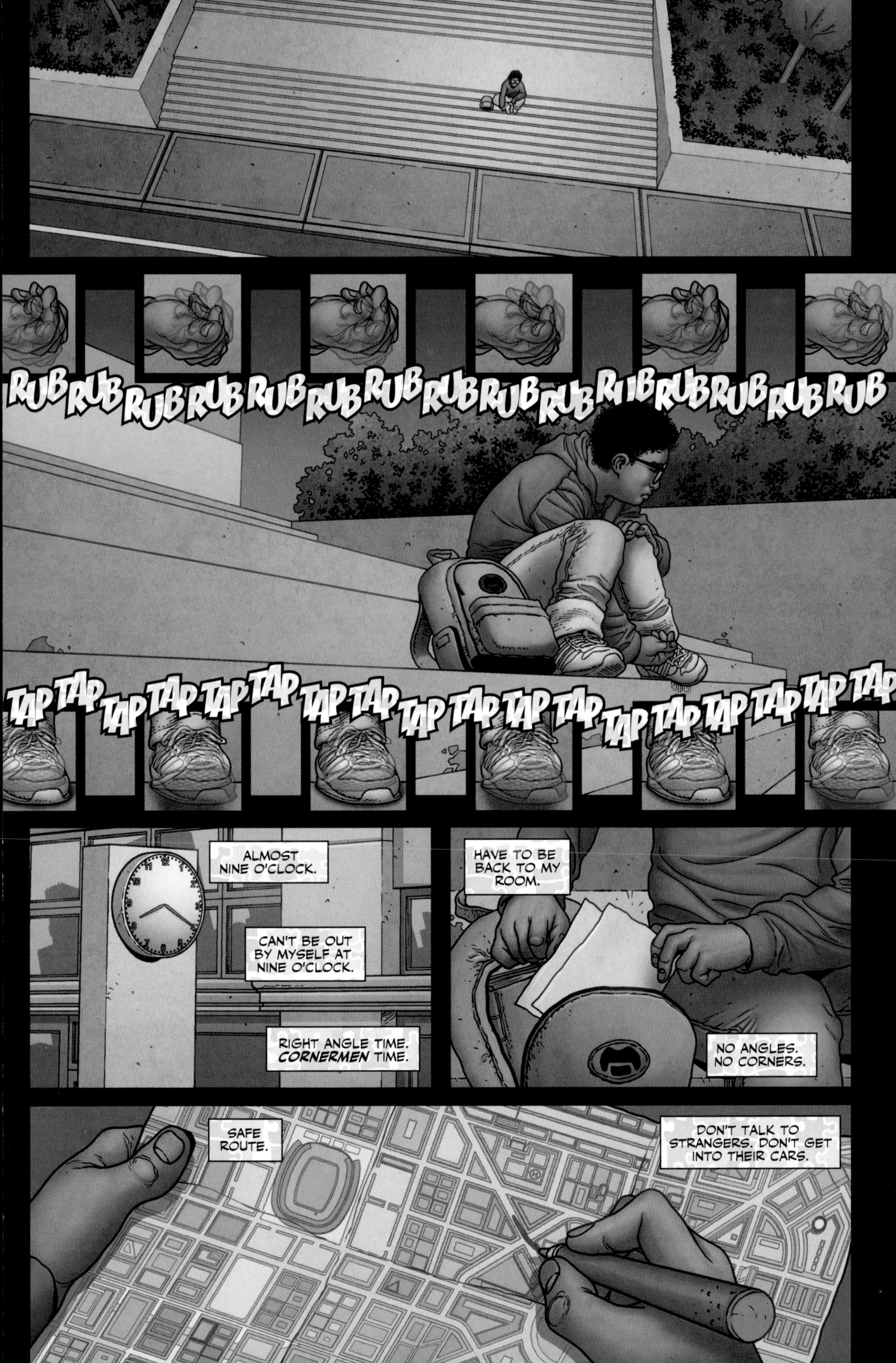
RUB RUB RUB RUB RUB RUB RUB RUB RUB RUB RI IB RUB RUB RUB RUB
TAP TAP TAP TAP TAP TAP TAP TAP TAP TAP TAP TAP TAP TAP TAP TAP TAP TAP
ALMOST NINE O'CLOCK.
CAN'T BE OUT BY MYSELF AT NINE O'CLOCK.
RIGHT ANGLE TIME. *CORNERMEN* TIME.
HAVE TO BE BACK TO MY ROOM.
NO ANGLES. NO CORNERS.
SAFE ROUTE.
DON'T TALK TO STRANGERS. DON'T GET INTO THEIR CARS.

WHY?
BECAUSE. THEY'LL DO STUFF TO YOU.
TK TK TK
REALLY?
YEAH, I'M OLDER, I, LIKE, KNOW STUFF.
STOP ASKING QUESTIONS. STEPHEN AND I ARE TRYING TO TEXT.
TK TK TK
I CAN PASS.
I CAN PASS.
I AM PASSING.
JUST A NORMAL KID ON HIS WAY HOME.
WALKING HOME PERFECTLY NORMALLY.

WHUMMMMP
UM... GUYS? THE ALARM?
WAIT FOR IT...
BRIIIINNNNNNGGGGGIIIIINNNNNNGGGGG
FALSE ALARM. BETTER CALL IT IN.
NO, I DON'T SEE ANYTHING, IT MUST HAVE BEEN A POSSUM OR SOMETHING. GONNA SHUT IT DOWN ON MY END, YEAH...

GO CASTLEMEN!
Heh.

BUMDUM
MOMOO
DUMDUMM
WHAT IS THIS STUFF?
IT'S MOMOO.
IT'S AMAZING.
MOMOO energy drink
IT'S THE DIRTY LOVE CHILD OF FIVE-HOUR ENERGY AND CHOCOLATE MILK.
I MEAN, IF YOU DIDN'T GET ANY SLEEP, OR YOU'RE CRAMMING, OR YOU'VE GOT TO DO THAT PRESIDENT'S FITNESS THING AND RUN AROUND THE TRACK FOREVER...
"IT'S GOT WHAT KIDS NEED!"
THIS IS MIND CONTROL.
THE ONLY QUESTION IS WHY YOU ARE BEING MIND CONTROLLED.
WHAT? NO. THAT'S CRAZY TALK!
I'M FAR TOO INDEPENDENT TO ALLOW MYSELF TO BE MANIPULATED.

YOU WERE NOT JOKING ABOUT THE SOPHISTICATION OF THIS LAB EQUIPMENT.
WE'VE NEVER SEEN ANYTHING LIKE IT.
OR *CONCEIVED* OF ANYTHING LIKE IT.
WELL WE DO GET ALL THE CUTTING-EDGE CRAP HERE...
NO. THIS IS NOT ON THE *"EDGE."*
THIS IS FAR, FAR BEYOND THE "EDGE."
AS IN THE FOUNDATIONAL TECHNOLOGY THAT NEEDS TO BE INVENTED *BEFORE* THIS CAN BE INVENTED HASN'T BEEN *INVENTED* YET.
THIS EQUIPMENT IS *LITERALLY* FROM THE *FUTURE.*
WHERE AND HOW DID ROOK *GET* THIS?

GET ME DOWN FROM HERE!
GET ME DOWN!
ARE YOU ALL RIGHT?
AM I ALL RIGHT? AM I ALL RIGHT?
DID YOU SERIOUSLY JUST ASK ME THAT QUESTION?
WHERE DID THEY GO?
CASTLES
THE SCHOOL, I'M PRETTY SURE THEY WENT TO THE SCHOOL, AND--
WAIT! WAIT! COME BACK HERE!
MY FATHER IS GONNA HEAR ABOUT THIS!
I WILL HAVE YOUR JOB, SHERMAN!
YOUR GOTH FREAK BRAT IS THE ONE WHO'S BEHIND ALL THIS!

YO! ZYGOSES.
NOK NOK
WE'RE ABOUT TO HAVE COMPANY.
READY TO BOOGIE?
HARDLY.
HOLD THEM OFF FOR APPROXIMATELY... FIFTEEN MINUTES, PLEASE.
FIFTEEN MINUTES. OKAY, "FOBBITS," WHATEVER YOU SAY.
DONK DONK DONK
YO, BABY. PUT DOWN YOUR BABY STUFF.
TIME TO DANCE.

GO CASTLEMEN!
TWINS SAY THEY NEED FIFTEEN.
GOOD. I'M CURIOUS TO SEE IF THEIR TECH LIVES UP TO THE HYPE...
...BY CRACKING IT OPEN AND SEEING WHAT'S ON THE INSIDE.
FIVE.
FOUR.
THREE.
TWO...
WHOOMWHOOMWHOOMWHOOMWHOOM

WHAT THE HECK WAS THAT?!
DADDY'S HOME.
REALLY?
"DID HE GET MY MESSAGE ABOUT KWAME?"

AVOIDING STORM DRAINS.
NO GOOD.
KEISHA SAID:
STAY AWAY FROM THEM, YOU'LL GET SUCKED INTO THE SEWER AND YOU'LL NEVER GET THE POOP STINK OFF.
TK TK TK
AVOIDING STREET LAMPS.
NO GOOD.
KEISHA SAID:
YOU HATE BUGS, RIGHT? THEY'RE ATTRACTED TO THE LIGHT.
STAY AWAY FROM STREET LAMPS AND YOU'LL COMPLAIN TO ME LESS.
TK TK TK
ALMOST THERE.
ALMOST THERE.
TIME IS EIGHT FORTY.
THAT'S ABOUT A 30 DEGREE ANGLE. NOT NINETY.
TOOK A SAFE ROUTE.
TAKES LONGER THAN IT SHOULD BECAUSE IT'S ALL SWERVES, NO CORNERS.
SAFE...

CHROME FEWER MEOW...

...LEATHER EWE *MUSK!*

KEISHA!
WHY WERE YOU LATE KEISHA?
KEISHA!
ROOK
WE ARE THE FUTURE

VALIANT

FRED VAN LENTE | FRANCIS PORTELA | DIEGO BERNARD
ANDREW DALHOUSE | BRIAN REBER

GENERATION ZERO

ROOK HIGH SCHOOL,
LAZARUS LANE SE.

LISTEN UP IN THERE!

THIS IS THE ROOK SHERIFF'S DEPARTMENT.

WE KNOW YOU'RE THERE.

YOU ARE WANTED FOR *KIDNAPPING.*

CRIMINAL TRESPASS.

BREAKING AND ENTERING.

VANDALIZING PUBLIC PROPERTY--

ATTENTION, ROOK'S SHERIFF'S DEPARTMENT!

THIS IS GENERATION ZERO.

YOU ARE WANTED BY US FOR CRIMES AGAINST THE FUTURE.
YOU ARE INTERFERING WITH AN INDEPENDENT CITIZENS' INVESTIGATION.
KID--YOU AND YOUR LITTLE FRIENDS BETTER COME DOWN FROM THERE--
--WITH YOUR HANDS UP, THEN LIE DOWN ON YOUR STOMACH, AND LACE YOUR FINGERS BEHIND YOUR HEA--
YOU MEN LAY DOWN YOUR ARMS, STEP OUT OF THE POWER ARMOR, AND WE WILL IMMOBILIZE YOU IN THE MOST HUMANE WAY POSSIBLE.
IF YOU RESIST ARREST--
IF YOU REMAIN HOSTILE, I CANNOT BE RESPONSIBLE FOR YOUR WELL-BEING.
NO MORE GAMES! THIS IS NOT A NEGOTIATION.
WE ARE NOT EQUALS!
YOU ARE CHILDREN.

AND YOU WILL OBEY.

SHRKKK

HOLD YOUR FIRE!
HOLD--

YEAH, THE SNIPER CIRCLING OVERHEAD WAS A REAL GOOD SIGN OF YOUR PEACEFUL INTENTIONS, SHERIFF!
THIS IS YOUR LAST CHANCE TO WALK AWAY!
TRUST ME-- YOU'RE NOT BEING PAID ENOUGH FOR THIS!

ENOUGH OF THIS! PLAYTIME'S OVER!
HIT 'EM WITH THE RADIANCE!

NOW-- WHILE THEY'RE BLINDED--
MOVE IN!
NON-LETHAL ONLY, SIR?

WHAT? HELL YEAH, NON-LETHAL, FOOL!
THEY'RE STILL JUST KIDS, DEPUTY!
CLOUD...?
CRONUS.
ARE WE NET-WORKED?
WE ARE NET-WORKED.
WE CAN "SEE" THEM...
...THROUGH MY PSYCHIC IMPRESSIONS OF THEM FROM COLLECTIVE CONSCIOUS-NESS.
ALL RIGHT ALL RIGHT ALL RIGHT...

GET WOKE, FASCISTS!
KKKKKKRRNNNCH
GGAAAAAAAHHH! GET IT OFF ME! GET IT OFF!

ROOK CITY HALL, FOUNDERS SQUARE.
ROOK
‹YES, AS YOU CAN SEE, MR. DEFENSE MINISTER, THE RADIANCE MODULES CAUSE COMPLETE VISUAL FAILURE FOR UP TO EIGHT HOURS--›
‹--YES, THAT IS A STANDARD FEATURE IN EVERY RRRIOT GEAR ARMOR...›
‹ABSOLUTELY. GREAT TO HEAR. LET ME TRANSFER YOU TO OUR SALES DEPARTMENT...›
DADDY!
HEY, BABY GIRL! GREAT TO SEE THE FIRE DEPARTMENT GOT YOU DOWN FROM LOOKOUT TOWER!
DADDY'S SUPER-HAPPY TO SEE YOU'RE STILL ALIVE BUT HE'S ALSO SUPER-BUSY RIGHT NOW.
IT'S PAST MIDNIGHT IN MICHIGAN BUT PRIME BUYING TIME IN MANY DICTATORSHIPS, ADELE.
THIS LIVESTREAM OF THE BATTLE WITH THE ZEROES HAS NEARLY DOUBLED ROOK DEFENSE CONCEPT'S QUARTERLY SALES IN UNITS...
I DON'T CARE.
I DON'T CARE ABOUT ANY OF THAT. IT DOESN'T MATTER.
UH-HUH. YEAH, THAT'S REALLY INTERESTING...
CASTLES

DADDY. I NEED YOU TO LISTEN TO ME.
BABY--BABY! I DON'T WANT TO SAY I WILL HAVE YOU RETROACTIVELY ABORTED IF YOU DON'T LEAVE RIGHT NOW...
...BUT THE PENTAGON IS CALLING.
THE PENTAGON OF THE UNITED STATES.
OF AMERICA?
THEY SPEND LIKE DRUNKEN KARDASHIANS ON WEAPONRY. THEY WILL MAKE US SO, SO SOOOOOO MUCH MONEY...
AND YOU CAN TALK TO THEM, ONCE YOU LISTEN TO THIS:
I KNOW WHAT I WANT FOR MY BIRTHDAY.
CASTLES
WHA...WHAT? I THOUGHT--I THOUGHT YOU WANTED THAT TRIP FOR ALL THE KEYS CLUB TO THE RESORT IN CABO--
SCREW CABO.
I HATE CABO!
I CHANGED MY MIND. FOR MY EIGHTEENTH BIRTHDAY...
...I WANT SUPER-POWERS.

ROOK HIGH.

WHY DO I FEEL LIKE WHENEVER YOU TWO *ZYGOS TWINS* ARE LOOKING AT ME IT'S LIKE YOU'RE STRIPPING ME WITH YOUR EYES?

UGH. QUITE THE CONTRARY, KEISHA SHERMAN.
WE FIND THE NAKED HUMAN FORM THOROUGHLY REPULSIVE.
WHEN WE LOOK AT YOU WE ARE TRYING OUR BEST TO PICTURE YOU WITH *MORE CLOTHES ON.*
DO ME A FAVOR.
BE LESS WEIRD.

GEEZ! AND COULD YOU HURRY UP SO WE CAN GET OUT OF HERE? SOUNDS LIKE A WARZONE OUT THERE!

AT LAST!
I HOPE... I HOPE MY DAD'S OKAY...
AND CRONUS.

I WANNA TEST IT!
NO ME!
NO WAY, YOU GOT TO INJECT YOURSELF FIRST LAST TIME!
NOBODY'S TESTING JACK UNTIL YOU TELL ME WHAT YOU'VE COOKED UP HERE.
REMEMBER WHAT WE LEARNED IN ADELE'S HEROSCAPE?
STEPHEN RECENTLY DEVELOPED A LACTOSE INTOLERANCE.
SO HE HAD TO STOP DRINKING MOMOO.
MOMOO, A PRODUCT OF THE ROOK BOTTLING COMPANY.
MOMOO, AVAILABLE FOR FREE AT EVERY VENDING MACHINE AT EVERY CORRIDOR JUNCTION AT EVERY ROOK SCHOOL.
MOMOO, WHICH OUR ANALYSIS SHOWS CONTAINS AN ENZYME DESIGNED TO SUPPRESS UNIQUE BRAIN FUNCTIONS IN ADOLESCENTS.
OUR ENZYME WILL ENHANCE THOSE UNIQUE BRAN FUNCTIONS INSTEAD, SO WE CAN SEE WHAT THEY'RE TRYING TO HIDE--
WHAT DO YOU MEAN, "UNIQUE BRAIN FUNCTIONS?" LIKE WHAT YOU ZEROES CAN DO?
NO, NO. AS THE HUMAN ANIMAL DEVELOPS, THE BRAINS OF EVEN NON-PSIOTS ARE IN A VERY DIFFERENT STAGE, PHYSICALLY, IN ADOLESCENCE THAN EITHER CHILD OR ADULT BRAINS.
THE ARTIFICIAL ENZYMES IN MOMOO SUPPRESS THESE FUNCTIONALITIES...
...BUT ONCE STEPHEN STOPPED DRINKING IT, HIS "TEEN BRAIN" BEGAN TO RETURN...
HE DID SAY... HE FELT LIKE HE COULD SEE "THROUGH" THE TOWN...

"...LIKE IT WAS FAKE
OR SOMETHING...
"...AND HE WAS BEING
DRAWN TO THE RUNOFF POND
BEYOND BISHOP'S WOODS...
"...IN HIS *DREAMS,* HE
SAID ON HIS RECORDING...
"...IT WAS
CALLING
TO HIM...
"...BUT WAS
IT A TRAP?"

DOUBTFUL. MORE LIKELY: AS IT IS THE *TOWN* THAT IS FEEDING ITS TEENAGERS MOMOO TO *HIDE* WHATEVER STEPHEN LEARNED...
...HE MADE HIS WAY TO THE *SLURRY POND* TO ACT ON THIS KNOWLEDGE, WAS *INTERCEPTED,* AND...
KEISHA?
WHO--?

YOU WERE LATE COMING TO GET ME, KEISHA.
WHY WERE YOU LATE?
KWAME-?!

NOW I DON'T KNOW WHERE I AM. BUT IT *HURTS.*

WHEN ARE YOU COMING TO GET ME, KEISHA?

HOW DID YOU GET HERE--HOW--

EEEEEEEEEEEAAAAAGGGGGH

REINFORCEMENT HOOPS TOURIST.

SAVE US, KEISHA SHERMAN!

YES, PROTECT US, KEISHA SHERMAN!

EATER HUE *WET FUR.*

HELL ARE YOU EVEN SUPPOSED TO BE, ANIMALIA?!
DON'T CALL ME THAT, COMMANDER!
I'M NOT JUST INTO BABY ANIMAL CARTOONS!
I LIKE MANGA AND STUFF NOW!
I'M ANIME-LIA!
SHERIFF, YOU SAID THEY'D BE BLINDED--
KRAKK
NGGHHA!

THESE AIN'T NO GODDAMN KIDS, SHERIFF! YOU'RE CRAZY!
LOOK AT IT! IT'S A MONSTER!
NO--THAT'S JUST--SOME KIND OF--SHELL AROUND HER--
--SWITCH YOUR VISUAL TO THE PSYCHOMAGNETIC SPECTRUM--YOU'LL SEE HER--
FORGET IT, KEITH! I'M NOT GOING HOME IN A BAG BECAUSE YOU CAN'T HANDLE BAD PRESS!
GOING FULL LETHAL! NO HOLDS BARRED!
GODDAMMIT NO CECIL I GAVE YOU AN--
BRAKKATA
BRAKKATA
BRAKKATA
BRAKKATA
WUNKKOOWWW
NNNN--!
CHOOOM
CHOOOOOM
CHOOOOOM
CHOOOOM
CHOOOOOOOOM

GUH...
NO! NO!
YOU IDIOT!
SSHRAAKKAKKOOOOOOOM
YOU WANNA GO FULL LETHAL?
YEAH, OKAY, SHERIFF!
AAAGGHH!
Nnnf
LET'S GO FULL LETHAL!

I'M SO *SICK* OF YOU WEIRDOS!

SUCK IT, EGGHEAD!

FWWOOOOOOSH

YEH!

WHERE DO YOU THINK YOU'RE GOING?!
THE ONLY WAY OUTTA THIS PLACE IS THROUGH *ME,* YOU--
HUGE NOSE ION!
JAMES! HELP!

--OR NOT.
RIGHT, THEY'RE CALLED "CORNER" MEN FOR A ***REASON.***

I-- I CANNOT SENSE KATY ANYWHERE ANYMORE, KEISHA SHERMAN--NOT AT ALL!
THAT IS A VERY BAD THING, KEISHA SHERMAN.
YOU DON'T NEED TO TELL ME TWICE.
C'MON, LET'S FIND THE OTHERS!

SHRAKKKKKK
YOU--
--YOU FILTH!
UNNNH!
YOU TRY TO CONTROL US--
--WITH FEAR--WITH PAIN--
WELL HOW YOU FEELIN' NOW, HUH?!
DO IT, CRONUS.
DO IT!
CRONUS! STOP!
WE GOT WHAT WE CAME FOR!
JUST LEAVE MY DAD ALONE!
THIS WORLD WE WERE BORN INTO--THIS HELL.
THEY CREATED IT.

I KNOW.
THAT'S WHY WE HAVE TO BE *BETTER.*
OR NOTHING *CHANGES!*
C'MON, CRONUS. I KNOW YOU *SEE* THAT...
...THERE'S STILL A *KID* SOMEWHERE INSIDE YOU, RIGHT...?
A KID THAT HAS *HOPE?*
KEISHA, LOOK OUT!

AAHHH!
CHUM
CHUM
CHUM
CHUM
CHUM
CHUM
CHUM
CHUM
CHUM
CHUM
CHUM

SHRRRAAAKKKKKK

TELIC, OH MY GOD... TELIC...
UNNGH... I KNEW THAT WAS GONNA HAPPEN... KOF!
BUT... BUT I DID IT ANYWAY...
WHY?!
GUESS... I KNOW... WHAT... HE SEES IN YOU... EVEN THOUGH...
...YOU'RE SO... DISTRESSINGLY... NORMAL, SHERMAN... KOF!
CRONUS! THEY GOT KATY! WE'VE GOT TO FIND HER! I DON'T SENSE HER PRESENCE!
ONE THING AT A TIME, JAMES...
COMMANDER.
THE MICHIGAN STATE POLICE ARE EN ROUTE. THEY WILL BE HERE IN APPROXIMATELY THREE MINUTES. I RECOMMEND EVAC...

SKREEEEEEE
...NOW! C'MON! GET IN!
GAMETE, WHAT THE HELL?
YOU HOTWIRED MY CAR?!
KEISHA-- DON'T.
DON'T GO WITH THEM.
PLEASE.
SORRY, DAD.
THIS IS MY NEW FAMILY.

HEAD BACK TO THE SLURRY POND IN BISHOP'S WOODS...
WE ALREADY SEARCHED THERE, KEISHA, AND CAME UP WITH NOTHING.
AND TELIC-- SHE'S LOST A LOT OF BLOOD. WE'VE GOT TO DO SOMETHING ABOUT THAT--
AND WE WILL. I JUST...
I HAVE TO KNOW.
I HAVE TO SEE WHAT STEPHEN WAS SEEING.
PPPPFFFFT
HRM.
NOT EVEN BUZZED.
WHAT WAS THAT SUPPOSED TO...
MY GOD.
PULL OVER! GAMETE, PULL OVER!
YOU...YOU CAN'T SEE THAT? REALLY?
NO-- WHAT IS IT? IS IT THE POND?
NO. THE SLURRY POND-- THAT'S THE SECRET.

THERE IS NO POND.
NEXT: HEROSCAPE

GENERATION ZERO #1 VARIANT COVER
Art by CLAYTON HENRY with ULISES ARREOLA

GENERATION ZERO
Character designs by ANDRÉS GUINALDO

GENERATION ZERO #2 COVER B
Art by TOM MULLER

GENERATION ZERO #3 VARIANT COVER
Art by DAN PARENT

GENERATION ZERO #4 VARIANT COVER
Art by JEFFREY VEREGGE

GENERATION ZERO #5 VARIANT COVER
Art by STEPHEN SEGOVIA

GENERATION ZERO #1, p.26
Art by FRANCIS PORTELA

GENERATION ZERO #1, p.27
Art by FRANCIS PORTELA

GENERATION ZERO #2, p.19
Art by FRANCIS PORTELA

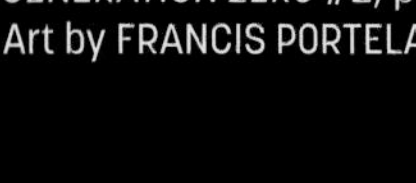
GENERATION ZERO #2, p.22
Art by FRANCIS PORTELA

GENERATION ZERO #4, p.3
Art by FRANCIS PORTELA

GENERATION ZERO #5, p.6
Art by FRANCIS PORTELA

GENERATION ZERO #5, p.13
Art by FRANCIS PORTELA

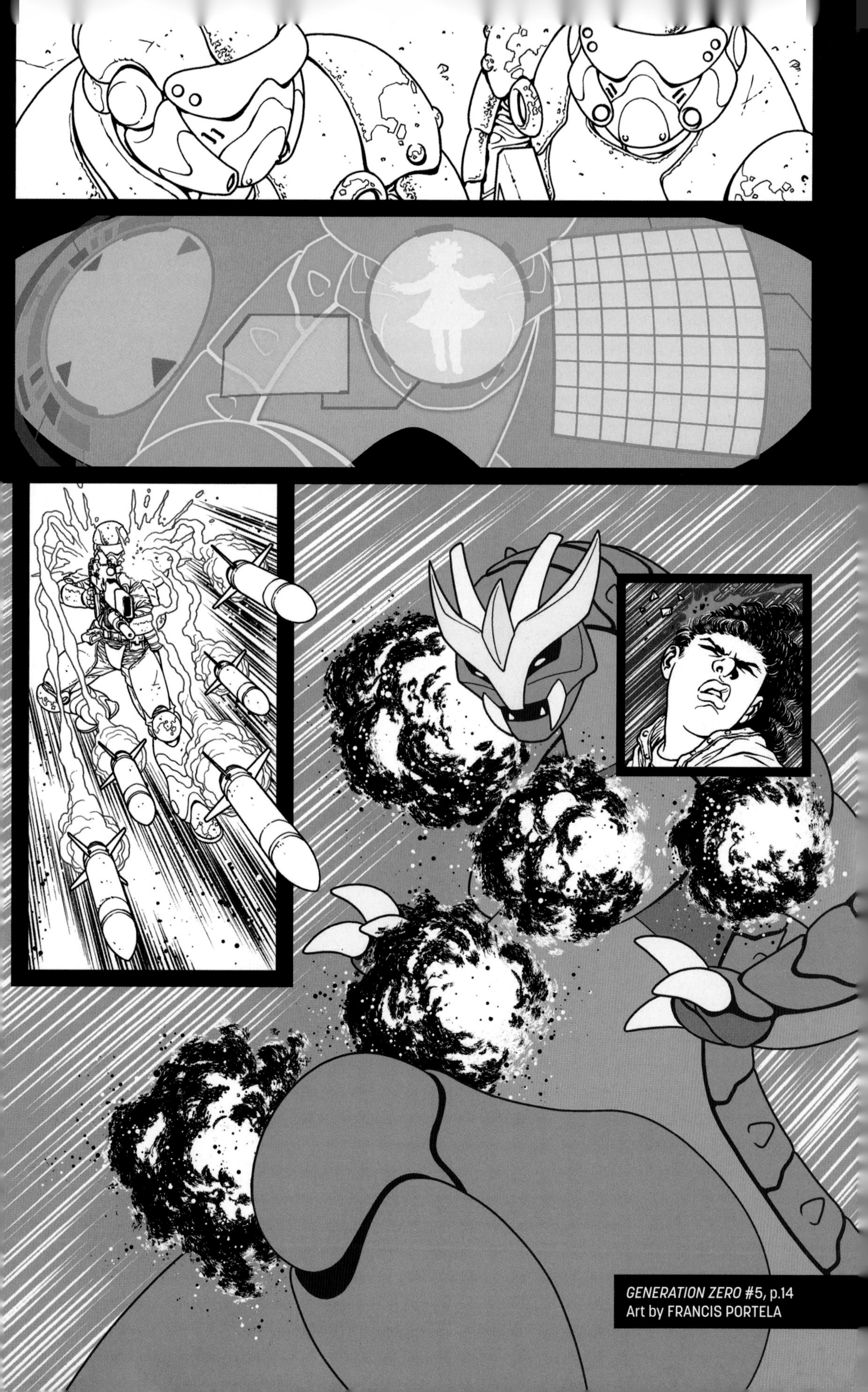

GENERATION ZERO #5, p.14
Art by FRANCIS PORTELA

EXPLORE THE VALIANT UNIVERSE

4001 A.D.

4001 A.D.
ISBN: 9781682151433

4001 A.D.: Beyond New Japan
ISBN: 9781682151464

Rai Vol 4: 4001 A.D.
ISBN: 9781682151471

A&A: THE ADVENTURES OF ARCHER AND ARMSTRONG

Volume 1: In the Bag
ISBN: 9781682151495

Volume 2: Romance and Road Trips
ISBN: 9781682151716

ARCHER & ARMSTRONG

Volume 1: The Michelangelo Code
ISBN: 9780979640988

Volume 2: Wrath of the Eternal Warrior
ISBN: 9781939346049

Volume 3: Far Faraway
ISBN: 9781939346148

Volume 4: Sect Civil War
ISBN: 9781939346254

Volume 5: Mission: Improbable
ISBN: 9781939346353

Volume 6: American Wasteland
ISBN: 9781939346421

Volume 7: The One Percent and Other Tales
ISBN: 9781939346537

ARMOR HUNTERS

Armor Hunters
ISBN: 9781939346452

Armor Hunters: Bloodshot
ISBN: 9781939346469

Armor Hunters: Harbinger
ISBN: 9781939346506

Unity Vol. 3: Armor Hunters
ISBN: 9781939346445

X-O Manowar Vol. 7: Armor Hunters
ISBN: 9781939346476

BLOODSHOT

Volume 1: Setting the World on Fire
ISBN: 9780979640964

Volume 2: The Rise and the Fall
ISBN: 9781939346032

Volume 3: Harbinger Wars
ISBN: 9781939346124

Volume 4: H.A.R.D. Corps
ISBN: 9781939346193

Volume 5: Get Some!
ISBN: 9781939346315

Volume 6: The Glitch and Other Tales
ISBN: 9781939346711

BLOODSHOT REBORN

Volume 1: Colorado
ISBN: 9781939346674

Volume 2: The Hunt
ISBN: 9781939346827

Volume 3: The Analog Man
ISBN: 9781682151334

Volume 4: Bloodshot Island
ISBN: 9781682151952

BOOK OF DEATH

Book of Death
ISBN: 9781939346971

Book of Death: The Fall of the Valiant Universe
ISBN: 9781939346988

DEAD DROP

ISBN: 9781939346858

THE DEATH-DEFYING DOCTOR MIRAGE

Volume 1
ISBN: 9781939346490

Volume 2: Second Lives
ISBN: 9781682151297

THE DELINQUENTS

ISBN: 9781939346513

DIVINITY

Volume 1
ISBN: 9781939346766

Volume 2
ISBN: 9781682151518

ETERNAL WARRIOR

Volume 1: Sword of the Wild
ISBN: 9781939346209

Volume 2: Eternal Emperor
ISBN: 9781939346292

Volume 3: Days of Steel
ISBN: 9781939346742

WRATH OF THE ETERNAL WARRIOR

Volume 1: Risen
ISBN: 9781682151235

Volumel 2: Labyrinth
ISBN: 9781682151594

FAITH

Faith Vol 1: Hollywood and Vine
ISBN: 9781682151402

Faith Vol 2: California Scheming
ISBN: 9781682151631

HARBINGER

Volume 1: Omega Rising
ISBN: 9780979640957

Volume 2: Renegades
ISBN: 9781939346025

Volume 3: Harbinger Wars
ISBN: 9781939346117

Volume 4: Perfect Day
ISBN: 9781939346155

Volume 5: Death of a Renegade
ISBN: 9781939346339

Volume 6: Omegas
ISBN: 9781939346384

HARBINGER WARS

Harbinger Wars
ISBN: 9781939346094

Bloodshot Vol. 3: Harbinger Wars
ISBN: 9781939346124

Harbinger Vol. 3: Harbinger Wars
ISBN: 9781939346117

IMPERIUM

Volume 1: Collecting Monsters
ISBN: 9781939346759

Volume 2: Broken Angels
ISBN: 9781939346896

Volume 3: The Vine Imperative
ISBN: 9781682151112

Volume 4: Stormbreak
ISBN: 9781682151372

NINJAK

Volume 1: Weaponeer
ISBN: 9781939346667

Volume 2: The Shadow Wars
ISBN: 9781939346940

Volume 3: Operation: Deadside
ISBN: 9781682151259

Volume 4: The Siege of King's Castle
ISBN: 9781682151617

QUANTUM AND WOODY

Volume 1: The World's Worst Superhero Team
ISBN: 9781939346186

Volume 2: In Security
ISBN: 9781939346230

Volume 3: Crooked Pasts, Present Tense
ISBN: 9781939346391

Volume 4: Quantum and Woody Must Die!
ISBN: 9781939346629

QUANTUM AND WOODY BY PRIEST & BRIGHT

Volume 1: Klang
ISBN: 9781939346780

Volume 2: Switch
ISBN: 9781939346803

Volume 3: And So...
ISBN: 9781939346865

Volume 4: Q2 - The Return
ISBN: 9781682151099

RAI

Volume 1: Welcome to New Japan
ISBN: 9781939346414

Volume 2: Battle for New Japan
ISBN: 9781939346612

Volume 3: The Orphan
ISBN: 9781939346841

Rai Vol 4: 4001 A.D.
ISBN: 9781682151471

SHADOWMAN

Volume 1: Birth Rites
ISBN: 9781939346001

Volume 2: Darque Reckoning
ISBN: 9781939346056

Volume 3: Deadside Blues
ISBN: 9781939346162

Volume 4: Fear, Blood, And Shadows
ISBN: 9781939346278

Volume 5: End Times
ISBN: 9781939346377

SHADOWMAN BY ENNIS & WOOD

ISBN: 9781682151358

IVAR, TIMEWALKER

Volume 1: Making History
ISBN: 9781939346636

Volume 2: Breaking History
ISBN: 9781939346834

Volume 3: Ending History
ISBN: 9781939346995

UNITY

Volume 1: To Kill a King
ISBN: 9781939346261

Volume 2: Trapped by Webnet
ISBN: 9781939346346

Volume 3: Armor Hunters
ISBN: 9781939346445

Volume 4: The United
ISBN: 9781939346544

Volume 5: Homefront
ISBN: 9781939346797

Volume 6: The War-Monger
ISBN: 9781939346902

Volume 7: Revenge of the Armor Hunters
ISBN: 9781682151136

THE VALIANT

ISBN: 9781939346605

VALIANT ZEROES AND ORIGINS

ISBN: 9781939346582

X-O MANOWAR

Volume 1: By the Sword
ISBN: 9780979640940

Volume 2: Enter Ninjak
ISBN: 9780979640995

Volume 3: Planet Death
ISBN: 9781939346087

Volume 4: Homecoming
ISBN: 9781939346179

Volume 5: At War With Unity
ISBN: 9781939346247

Volume 6: Prelude to Armor Hunters
ISBN: 9781939346407

Volume 7: Armor Hunters
ISBN: 9781939346476

Volume 8: Enter: Armorines
ISBN: 9781939346551

Volume 9: Dead Hand
ISBN: 9781939346650

Volume 10: Exodus
ISBN: 9781939346933

Volume 11: The Kill List
ISBN: 9781682151273

Volume 12: Long Live the King
ISBN: 9781682151655

X-O Manowar Vol. 13: Succession and Other Tales
ISBN: 9781682151754

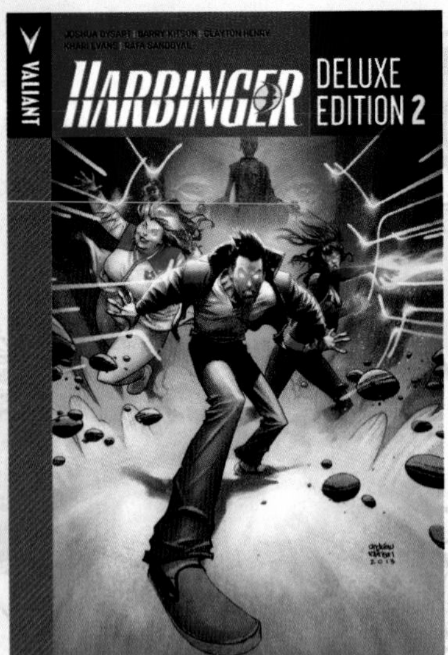

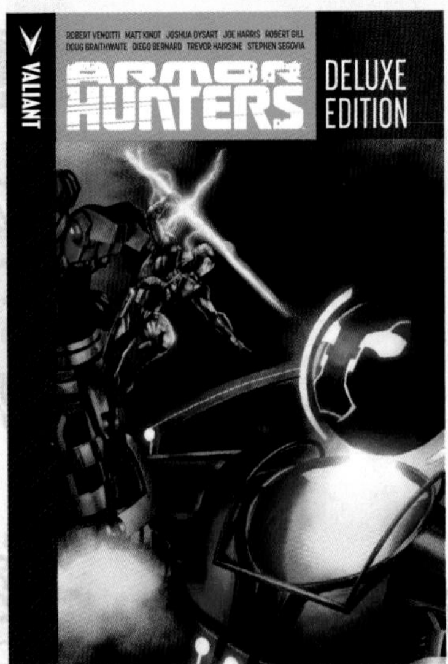

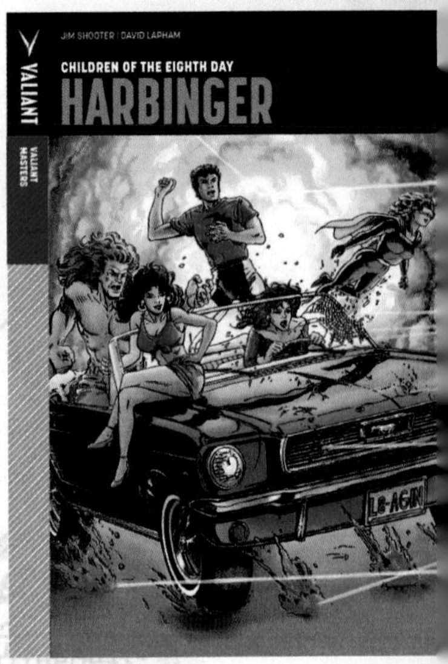

Omnibuses

Archer & Armstrong: The Complete Classic Omnibus
ISBN: 9781939346872
Collecting ARCHER & ARMSTRONG (1992) #0-26, ETERNAL WARRIOR (1992) #25 along with ARCHER & ARMSTRONG: THE FORMATION OF THE SECT.

Quantum and Woody: The Complete Classic Omnibus
ISBN: 9781939346360
Collecting QUANTUM AND WOODY (1997) #0, 1-21 and #32, THE GOAT: H.A.E.D.U.S. #1, and X-O MANOWAR (1996) #16

X-O Manowar Classic Omnibus Vol. 1
ISBN: 9781939346308
Collecting X-O MANOWAR (1992) #0-30, ARMORINES #0, X-O DATABASE #1, as well as material from SECRETS OF THE VALIANT UNIVERSE #1

Deluxe Editions

Archer & Armstrong Deluxe Edition Book 1
ISBN: 9781939346223
Collecting ARCHER & ARMSTRONG #0-13

Archer & Armstrong Deluxe Edition Book 2
ISBN: 9781939346957
Collecting ARCHER & ARMSTRONG #14-25, ARCHER & ARMSTRONG: ARCHER #0 and BLOODSHOT AND H.A.R.D. CORPS #20-21.

Armor Hunters Deluxe Edition
ISBN: 9781939346728
Collecting Armor Hunters #1-4, Armor Hunters: Aftermath #1, Armor Hunters: Bloodshot #1-3, Armor Hunters: Harbinger #1-3, Unity #8-11, and X-O MANOWAR #23-29

Bloodshot Deluxe Edition Book 1
ISBN: 9781939346216
Collecting BLOODSHOT #1-13

Bloodshot Deluxe Edition Book 2
ISBN: 9781939346810
Collecting BLOODSHOT AND H.A.R.D. CORPS #14-23, BLOODSHOT #24-25, BLOODSHOT #0, BLOODSHOT AND H.A.R.D. CORPS: H.A.R.D. CORPS #0, along with ARCHER & ARMSTRONG #18-19

Book of Death Deluxe Edition
ISBN: 9781682151150
Collecting BOOK OF DEATH #1-4, BOOK OF DEATH: THE FALL OF BLOODSHOT #1, BOOK OF DEATH: THE FALL OF NINJAK #1, BOOK OF DEATH: THE FALL OF HARBINGER #1, and BOOK OF DEATH: THE FALL OF X-O MANOWAR #1.

Divinity Deluxe Edition
ISBN: 97819393460993
Collecting DIVNITY #1-4

Harbinger Deluxe Edition Book 1
ISBN: 9781939346131
Collecting HARBINGER #0-14

Harbinger Deluxe Edition Book 2
ISBN: 9781939346773
Collecting HARBINGER #15-25, HARBINGER: OMEGAS #1-3, and HARBINGER: BLEEDING MONK #0

Harbinger Wars Deluxe Edition
ISBN: 9781939346322
Collecting HARBINGER WARS #1-4, HARBINGER #11-14, and BLOODSHOT #10-13

Ivar, Timewalker Deluxe Edition Book 1
ISBN: 9781682151198
Collecting IVAR, TIMEWALKER #1-12

Quantum and Woody Deluxe Edition Book 1
ISBN: 9781939346681
Collecting QUANTUM AND WOODY #1-12 and QUANTUM AND WOODY: THE GOAT #0

Q2: The Return of Quantum and Woody Deluxe Edition
ISBN: 9781939346568
Collecting Q2: THE RETURN OF QUANTUM AND WOODY #1-5

Rai Deluxe Edition Book 1
ISBN: 9781682151174
Collecting RAI #1-12, along with material from RAI #1 PLUS EDITION and RAI #5 PLUS EDITION

Shadowman Deluxe Edition Book 1
ISBN: 9781939346438
Collecting SHADOWMAN #0-10

Shadowman Deluxe Edition Book 2
ISBN: 9781682151075
Collecting SHADOWMAN #11-16, SHADOWMAN #13X, SHADOWMAN: END TIMES #1-3 and PUNK MAMBO #0

Unity Deluxe Edition Book 1
ISBN: 9781939346575
Collecting UNITY #0-14

The Valiant Deluxe Edition
ISBN: 97819393460986
Collecting THE VALIANT #1-4

X-O Manowar Deluxe Edition Book 1
ISBN: 9781939346100
Collecting X-O MANOWAR #1-14

X-O Manowar Deluxe Edition Book 2
ISBN: 9781939346520
Collecting X-O MANOWAR #15-22, and UNITY #1-4

X-O Manowar Deluxe Edition Book 3
ISBN: 9781682151310
Collecting X-O MANOWAR #23-29 and ARMOR HUNTERS #1-4.

Valiant Masters

Bloodshot Vol. 1 - Blood of the Machine
ISBN: 9780979640933

H.A.R.D. Corps Vol. 1 - Search and Destroy
ISBN: 9781939346285

Harbinger Vol. 1 - Children of the Eighth Day
ISBN: 9781939346483

Ninjak Vol. 1 - Black Water
ISBN: 9780979640971

Rai Vol. 1 - From Honor to Strength
ISBN: 9781939346070

Shadowman Vol. 1 - Spirits Within
ISBN: 9781939346018